THE SPECIAL ONES

THE SPECIAL ONES

TELENA LANDER

The Special Ones
Copyright © 2020 by Telena Lander

Library of Congress Control Number: 2020900774
ISBN-13:   Paperback: 978-1-64749-037-9
            ePub: 978-1-64749-038-6

All rights reserved. No part of this publication may be reproduced, distributed, or transmitted in any form or by any means, including photocopying, recording, or other electronic or mechanical methods, without the prior written permission of the publisher or author, except in the case of brief quotations embodied in critical reviews and certain other noncommercial uses permitted by copyright law.

Although every precaution has been taken to verify the accuracy of the information contained herein, the author and publisher assume no responsibility for any errors or omissions. No liability is assumed for damages that may result from the use of information contained within.

Printed in the United States of America

GoToPublish LLC
1-888-337-1724
www.gotopublish.com
info@gotopublish.com

CONTENTS

CHAPTER I 1
CHAPTER II 11
CHAPTER III 15
CHAPTER IV 19
CHAPTER V 21
CHAPTER VI 27
CHAPTER VII 29
CHAPTER VIII 37
CHAPTER IX 45
CHAPTER X 55
CHAPTER XI 65
CHAPTER XII 73
CHAPTER XIII 85
CHAPTER XIV 93
CHAPTER XV 103
CHAPTER XVI 111
CHAPTER XVII 115
CHAPTER XVIII 121
CHAPTER XIX 125
CHAPTER XX 143
CHAPTER XXI 153
CHAPTER XXII 157

CONTENTS

I dedicated the book to Crystal Merida, my husband, and the Weed Family.

CHAPTER 1

"Erica!" Erica's mom yelled to her daughter from upstairs. "Your ride is here."

"Coming!" Erica yelled to her mom while finishing the last touches of her makeup.

Erica had been waiting for this day to come. This was going to be her first group date. She was all excited about it.

Erica's date was Mike Summers. He had short brown hair and dark-green eyes. He was also tall and skinny. Erica and her mom thought Mike was cute. He was waiting for Erica in the den. Mike liked Erica a lot. He couldn't wait to get going.

Erica's mom was a pretty lady in her late thirties. Her name was Teria Lawrence. She had dark blonde hair and blue eyes. She was also very tall and slender. Teria even had some muscles since she did gymnastics when she was a teenager.

"Where are you all going?" Teria asked Mike.

"We are going to eat out and maybe catch a movie afterward," said Mike to Teria, wondering what was taking Erica so long.

"That sounds good," Teria said to Mike, happy that Mike was Erica's date. "I hope you all have a good time."

"I hope so," said Mike, thinking about what they were all going to do once they got going.

Teria liked Mike. She hoped that Erica and Mike would become good friends and that they would have a good time with their other friends tonight. It reminded her of her past, when she was a teenager.

"Erica has been trying to fast-forward this day to see you," Teria told Mike as Erica was coming downstairs.

"I sure have," said Erica, walking toward Mike and her mom in a lovely white and black dress covered with lace.

"Wow! You look beautiful," said Mike to Erica, about to blush.

"Thanks!" said Erica, smiling at Mike. "We better get going, Mom."

"You all have a good time now," Teria said, looking at her beautiful daughter and Mike beside her.

"We will," said Erica. Then Mike and Erica went out of her house and went to Mike's car.

Erica is growing up way too fast, Teria thought, while looking at her daughter walking beside Mike.

Mike's car was a Rodeo. The color of the car was black. Mike loved his car. Erica liked it too. She thought it was very nice. She wished that she had a car of her own to drive in. It was a shame that her parents couldn't afford a car for her to drive in back and forth from school, but that's the real world for her, anyway.

Mike and Erica left her house and went to pick up their friends. They talked about all kinds of stuff. One thing they talked about was karate. They both loved martial arts. As a matter of fact, Erica and Mike met at a karate school. It was right next to their high school. The karate school was called Don's Do Jo.

Erica and Mike were then at their friend's house. Their friend's name was Glenn. He had a very nice two-story home covered with white shingles and a brown roof. Flowers and trees of many kinds fill the yard next to the house. There was even a sidewalk to the front door. It was surrounded by dandelions and the most beautiful rose bushes anyone had ever seen. By the beautiful garden, you could tell that one of the people in Glenn's house had to be a gardener, which happen to be his mom, Claire.

Mike and Erica followed the path to the front door while looking at the beautiful scenery. Once they had reached the front door, Mike lifted up his arm and knocked on the wooden door with his hand.

Glenn answered the door. He had slick black hair. Glenn was not very tall, but he was skinny. He also had brown eyes and a nice tuxedo on. He was ready to go out and have some fun!

"Where is Ayla?" Erica and Mike asked Glenn.

"Ayla is still upstairs," Glenn said to Mike and Erica with a sigh. "She will be down in a minute, I hope."

Glenn was getting impatient on waiting for Ayla. She always had to be perfect. That was the only thing that Glenn did not like about her.

Oh well, you can't have everything you want from a girl, *Glenn thought to himself.*

Glenn was Ayla's date. They were good friends that live right next door to each other.

Ayla came down the stairs, dressed in beautiful blue satin and lace. She was finally ready to go on a group date with her friends.

"Let's go," said Ayla as she tapped Glenn on the shoulder to get his attention. Glenn turned around and looked at his gorgeous date.

"Wow!" said Glenn with embedded eyes. "No wonder it took you so long. You do look perfect!"

"Thanks!" said Ayla, pleased with herself.

"Okay," said Mike, trying to get his friends' attention. "Now that everyone is ready, let's get this group date started!" Then they went to his truck.

Once Mike got the car cranked up, he and his friends headed to a town called Boo pa. They thought the town was called Boo pa because most of the people in town loved to play practical jokes on other people, especially on tourists. Mike and his friends had to watch out for those people as they headed into town.

While they were traveling through the town, they came upon a restaurant. Mike and his friends stopped the car and decided to check the restaurant out. It was called the Wompa Restaurant. *Wompa* means "watch out for practical jokers because they might stomp all over you."

Mike, Erica, Glenn, and Ayla walked into the restaurant, hoping that no practical jokers would see them, but unfortunately, one did. It was a man in a black suit. He had short black hair and dark-blue eyes. The man was a chubby fellow standing in a corner. The man watched them find a table.

Mike and his friends found a table by a window. They sat down and waited for a menu. After a few minutes passed, a waitress came by with some menus.

The waitress had blue eyes and long red hair. She also had a small dimple right under her mouth. The waitress was skinny and around twenty-five years old. She was wearing a white T-shirt and black pants. The waitress was smiling at Mike and his friends while hoping a practical joker would get them because she knew that would be a sight to see.

"My name is Ashley," said the waitress as she gave some menus to Mike and his friends. "I will be your waitress this evening. What would you like to drink?"

Mike and his friends thought for a minute, and then they told Ashley what they wanted. They ended up getting two iced teas and two cokes. After they told Ashley their beverages, she left to get their drinks while they looked over the menus.

There was a variety of different foods on the menu. From sandwiches to seafood, it all looked good to Mike and his friends.

While Mike and his friends were looking over their menus, the practical joker was still watching. He was just waiting for the right time to get them good. In the meantime, he found a table right next to them. After a few minutes had passed, the waitress came back. She had a little notepad and a pen in her hand.

"Are you ready to order?" Ashley asked.

"Yes, we are," said Glenn, looking at Ashley. "I want shrimp and oysters."

Ashley wrote down what Glenn wanted and asked the rest of his friends what they wanted to eat.

Once Ashley got the rest of their orders, she left the table to get their food.

"Are we going to watch a movie or something after we eat?" Erica asked Mike.

"We might, depends on what time we get out of this restaurant."

"Oh," said Erica, wondering if this group date was going to be as great as she wanted it to be. It had been so far, but she had a strange feeling that it wouldn't last. She had no idea of what was about to happen.

The practical joker saw that Mike and his friends were busy talking to each other. Here was his chance to surprise them good. He got the ketchup and mustard off the table he was sitting in and held them in his hands. He was ready to squirt Mike and his friends good. The practical joker couldn't wait to see the look on their faces when they got creamed.

The practical joker reached over the table and squirted the ketchup and mustard right over Mike's and Erica's heads onto Glenn's and Ayla's faces and clothes.

"Oh no!" exclaimed Glenn and Ayla with surprised looks on their faces.

"My tuxedo!" exclaimed Glenn, trying to wipe off the ketchup and mustard off his suit while looking for the culprit.

"My face, my dress!" exclaimed Ayla as she got a napkin and wiped off the ketchup and mustard off her clothes.

While all this was happening, Mike and Erica couldn't help themselves and started laughing at their friends who were all covered in ketchup and mustard.

"This isn't funny you guys!" said Ayla, getting mad at Mike and Erica. "Now the culprit has gotten away, thanks to you all giggling and not helping us!"

"We are sorry," said Mike, trying to stop laughing. "We just couldn't resist, especially with the mustard dripping off your beautiful black hair."

"I got mustard in my hair too!" exclaimed Ayla, surprised. "Just great! Now I got to wash my hair tonight! If I ever get my hands on that culprit, he is going to wish he never lived!"

"It is funny," said Glenn as he saw the mustard dripping from Ayla's hair.

They were all laughing now, except for Ayla, who was drenched in mustard and ketchup. She was really getting mad at her friends now.

"That practical joker got you good," exclaimed Glenn to Ayla while still trying to stop laughing.

"Shut up!" said Ayla, getting annoyed with her friends.

"Excuse me," said Ashley, interrupting their conversation. "Here is your food." Then Ashley realized what had happened to them.

"A practical joker got you all," said Ashley, about to laugh.

"Yes, one did," said Glenn to the waitress.

Ashley laughed and gave Glenn and his friends their food. Then Ashley left, wondering who was the practical joker that got them so good.

Mike, Glenn, and Erica told Ayla that they were sorry that they had laughed at her. Ayla forgave them.

"Let's eat and then get out of here while we still can," said Ayla, not wanting to never see another practical joker again.

Ayla's friends agreed with her as they started to eat their food.

Mike, Erica, Glenn, and Ayla enjoyed their meal together. When they finished their meals, Ashley came back with their ticket. Before she left them, she told them one last thing.

"I thought you might like to know how this town started with such a strange name since I noticed that this is the first time you have visited here," said Ashley to Ayla and her friends.

"We thought it was because of the practical jokers," said Erica, wondering if she was right.

"Yes, practical jokers is the main reason why the town is called Boo pa, but that's not all of it. Usually, after a practical joker got a person, he or she would say, 'Oops, I made a boo-boo.' And so people decided to call this town Boo pa, meaning 'I made a boo-boo.'"

"Okay," said Erica, "that does make sense."

"Thank you for telling us the history of this town," Glenn said while looking at Ashley.

"You're welcome," said Ashley, smiling. "Come back anytime."

"Sure," said Ayla, sarcastically.

Ayla had no intention of coming back to the Wompa Restaurant. She didn't want to get creamed by another practical joker. She hated the restaurant now.

Ayla and her friends told Ashley goodbye and went to pay for their meals. Then they left the restaurant and went to Mike's car.

At Mike's car, he and his friends were standing against the car, trying to figure out what they were going to do with the rest of their time together. Then Glenn suggested an idea.

"Why don't we head toward home. If we see something interesting, then we can stop and check it out?" Glenn asked his friends.

"That's a good idea," Ayla commented to Glenn.

"Well, okay then," said Mike. "Let's go!"

Glenn and his friends got back on the road. They hoped to find something to do with their time left together. Little did they know that wish was about to come true in a big way.

CHAPTER II

While Glenn and his friends were on the road, they talked and looked out the window of Mike's car, waiting for something interesting to happen. Erica was staring out the window, looking at the sky and trees. The stars were out, so she couldn't see much outside, but then something happened. She saw a bright beam of light go through the sky into some trees. The beam of light appeared to be coming from a meteorite. Erica wanted to see if it really was a meteorite that had fallen from outer space and landed on earth.

"Hey, you guys!" said Erica, wanting to check out the light. "Stop the car! I saw a beam of light go through some trees and crash down on the ground. Let's go see what it is!"

Mike stopped the car and got off the road. Then they got out of the car and looked at the woods. They all wondered what was out there waiting for them.

"Do you have a flashlight?" Erica asked Mike, seeing it was too dark to walk without one.

"Yes, it's in the trunk of the car."

Erica got the flashlight out of the trunk and cut it on. She looked at the woods. They looked spooky, but she was determined to find out what the light was that had fallen from the sky into the woods.

"Let's go!" Erica said to her friends, anxious to see what had fallen from the sky.

While Erica, Mike, Glenn, and Ayla were walking toward the thing that fell to the ground, they talked about what they might find.

"Do you think we will see something awesome? Like an alien from outer space?" Mike asked his friends around him curiously.

"I doubt it," said Ayla, not believing in superstitious stuff. "It's probably just a meteorite."

"I don't know. It might be a giant spaceship with an ugly big green alien in it, ready to take over the world," Glenn said, trying to scare his friends.

"Yeah right," said Erica, refusing to fall for Glenn's jokes. "And I am the wicked witch of the West."

"Okay, okay! You got me."

"Guys!" yelled Mike, trying to get Glenn's and Ayla's attention. "Let's just go and check it out. Then we will see who's right and who's wrong."

They all agreed with Mike and headed up a hill that took them deeper into the woods. Once they had reached the top of the hill, they saw the spot where the thing had landed. It was right below them. They all looked at it with wide eyes. They were stunned. They couldn't believe that they were looking at what seemed to be a real live spaceship that had fallen on earth from a distant planet millions of light-years away.

The spaceship was the color of gray. It had thousands of lights on it of all kinds of colors, but only one of them was on. There appeared to be no windows or doors on it.

There was a strange noise, and then something magical happened. A piece of the spaceship came apart and landed on the ground. The piece of the spaceship became a ramp to the UFO.

Mike and his friends watched the ramp come down as their mouth dropped open, stunned. They couldn't believe what they were seeing before their own eyes. It was like they were dreaming, but it was real.

"I told you so," said Glenn to his friends, the first one to speak, after seeing the U.F.O.

"Let's just hope they come in peace," said Erica, scared.

Erica and her friends dared not to move. They were too scared that something would jump out of the spaceship and kill them.

The ramp to the spaceship was on the ground now. Erica and her friends could now see inside the spaceship, but they couldn't see much from where they were standing. What they could see, though, was lots of lights and buttons of all colors. There were no aliens in sight, and they were relieved.

"Could the aliens be dead?" said Ayla, wondering.

"I don't know," said Erica, curious. "Why don't we go find out?"

"What!" exclaimed Glenn, surprised. "Are you crazy? Didn't you hear what I said about the aliens?"

"Yes," said Erica to Glenn, staring at her. "I just want to check it out. Come on, guys. Let's go see what is in this spaceship, or you chicken?" Erica said, about to imitate a chicken.

"No," said Glenn, trying to prove he was not a scaredy-cat.

"Let's go then," said Erica. So they walked slowly toward the UFO.

Erica had that dangerous look on her face. It showed how much she wanted to explore the spaceship. Could she be getting her friends and herself in trouble?

The closer Erica and her friends got to the spaceship, the more frightened they became at what they might find in the UFO. When they had reached the ramp, they stared at the spaceship, astounded. They now saw everything they had seen before, but at a closer look. The spaceship appeared to be made out of uranium. They saw that the lights circled all around the UFO and the spaceship itself was shaped between an oval and a square.

Then they had gotten up enough courage that they had reached the top of the ramp. They were now inside the spaceship, looking around. The spaceship was huge inside. There were buttons everywhere. Two big chairs were against the left wall. The colors of the buttons ranged from yellow to solid black. There was a big television screen above some buttons in the middle of the UFO. Erica and her friends thought that the aliens used this big television to see where they were going since there appeared to be no windows in the spaceship. They hadn't seen aliens—at least not yet. They wondered where they could be and if they were still alive, wandering around the spaceship, having no idea that intruders were among them. They didn't understand why they hadn't seen any, even though they weren't so sure if they wanted to.

Erica and her friends started searching around the UFO, hoping to find a sign of where the aliens were at that controlled, strange craft from outer space. They were scared but too intrigued to give up now. They had come too far. Who knows what lies ahead for Erica and her friends in the spaceship.

CHAPTER III

Mike was looking at the floor of the spaceship, trying to find the pilot of the strange craft. Then all of sudden, Mike saw something that scared him a little. He saw four bugs the size of two small bricks put together. In other words, it couldn't be from earth, or could it?

"Hey, guys, take a look at this!" yelled Mike, trying to get his friends' attention while looking down at the bugs.

Mike's friends went up to him to see what he had found. They gathered around the bugs and watched them. They dared not touch the bugs. Who knows what kind of poison or infection the bugs could give them, whether they wanted it or not.

The four bugs were looking at Mike and his friends. They were covered in all kinds of colors. Each was a little different from the others. In a way, they all looked like giant moths. They each had six legs. They appeared to be harmless to Mike and his friends. Then the strangest thing happened. One of the bugs spoke. The bug spoke in a strange language that Mike and his friends did not understand, a language they had never heard before and didn't know existed.

"What is the bug saying?" Glenn asked his friends.

"I have no clue," said Mike to Glenn, trying to figure out what foreign language the bug was speaking.

They didn't have any idea. They could only guess. Then the bug stopped talking, and all was quite. Twenty seconds had passed when they heard a noise coming from what seem to be outside the spaceship. They turned their heads toward the noise. When they did this, the four bugs sneaked up their legs and bit them.

"Get it off me!" Ayla screamed to Glenn while trying to shake the bug off.

Glenn couldn't help her because he was having the same problem.

"Ouch!" exclaimed Erica as one of the bugs bit her too.

"Let go!" said Mike, trying to get the strange-looking bug off his leg. Then all of a sudden, the bugs left Mike and his friends alone and flew away into the sky, where the stars were the brightest.

"Look!" said Ayla to her friends. "They're flying away."

Ayla and her friends watched the bugs fly out of the spaceship and into the dark sky. It was a sight to see.

"Hmmm, that's strange," said Glenn. "They all let go of us and flew away at the same time, as if something was calling them."

"It was bizarre," said Mike, agreeing with his friend.

"They were some neat-looking bugs, but they packed quite a bite," said Erica to her friends.

"No kidding," said Ayla, totally agreeing with Erica. Mike and Glenn nodded their heads with definite approval. They knew that they would never forget this night no matter what happened in the future.

"Let's get out of here before something else happens," said Glenn, ready to go home. He had had quite enough action for today, and so did the others. They agreed with him and left the spaceship, but they dared not leave without taking one last look at the spaceship before heading back to Mike's car. While they made their trip back to Mike's car, they all wondered what planet in space the strange spaceship came from.

CHAPTER IV

Mike and his friends were back in his car. They were thinking about the UFO. Mike was driving. He was relieved that they were all safe and that nothing really bad had happened while they were in the spaceship. There was one thing left that they were worried about though. It was the thought that the bugs might be poisonous or would give them some kind of infection. As matter of fact, they didn't feel very good. Were they just tired, or where they getting sick from the strange bugs that had bit them in the spaceship?

"Hey," said Glenn, thinking, "this could make us famous!"

"I don't know," said Mike, not sure. "Let's just keep this our secret for a while. Besides, nobody would probably believe us anyhow. They would think we were crazy or something."

"Yes, I guess you are right," said Glenn to Mike, disappointed.

Glenn and his friends were pretty quiet the rest of the way home. They were all tired from the adventure they just had together, especially Mike, who still couldn't believe what they had all seen. It seemed like a dream to him, even though he knew it was real. He had never believed in aliens until now. He finally got the chance to see for himself that people weren't lying when they say that they saw a strange craft floating through the sky. So Mike was now a believer, and the same goes for his friends.

Mike and Erica dropped off Ayla and Glenn at their houses. Ayla and Glenn told their friends they had a good time, except for getting creamed by the practical joker. Mike promised them that if they ever went on another group date together, they would go to a different town. Then Erica and Mike left their houses and went to Erica's house.

Once Erica got to her house, she kissed Mike good night. Mike blushed and told Erica he enjoyed their evening together. Erica agreed and told him good night.

Mike watched Erica go into her house. At that moment, Mike thought Erica was the prettiest girl he had ever seen. He was so glad to have her as a girlfriend. Mike loved everything about her and hoped that they would stay friends forever or maybe even get married one day and have kids, but that was too far in the future for now, anyway.

CHAPTER V

Erica and her friends had nightmares all night about the spaceship and getting bit by the strange bugs. They woke the next morning with sweat rolling down their faces and yawns from not getting much sleep. They had tossed and turned all night long, fighting their dreams.

The nightmares Erica and her friends had were all the same. They saw the bugs coming at them. The bugs or what had appeared to be giant moths were biting them like before, but this time, they wouldn't let go, and they kept on biting them until they died. They were so relieved that the dream wasn't real, but it felt as real as night and day to them.

When Erica and her friends got to school the next morning, they found out that they had dreamed basically the same nightmare, and they couldn't understand it. They promised themselves they would never go back to the spaceship after dreaming those awful nightmares. When they had promised each other that, they went on to their classes, trying to forget about last night.

Ayla was in class. She was listening to her teacher, Mrs. Hunter. A friend of hers was sitting beside her in a desk. Her name was Gabriell San. They had been friends since fourth grade. Gabriell was a popular girl in school. She had brown hair and blue-green eyes. She was also tall and slender. There were always boys staring at her, but they were too shy to ask her out. Some of them were cute, and some of them were ugly. One was staring at Gabriell right then.

The boy who was staring at Gabriell happen to be one of the ugly boys that had a crush on her. His name was Ralph. He had red hair and chubby cheeks. His eyes were dark green. Freckles covered his face. Ralph was wearing a green shirt with short sleeves. His stomach was hanging out of it. Seeing this, anybody could tell he was overweight. Ralph also had on a messy pair of jeans with holes in them.

Gabriell and Ayla thought the boy was gross, and they didn't like him at all. Ralph was like a big fat bully that loved to flirt with every cute girl in school. Knowing that, Ayla whispered into Gabriell's ear. She told her that Ralph was staring at her.

"I know," Gabriell whispered to Ayla while trying to ignore Ralph, who still had his eyes glued on her. "He always stares at me in class."

"He's probably got a crush on you," Ayla whispered to Gabriell, wanting to burst out laughing because of Ralph. She held it in for her friend's shake.

"I hope not. He certainly isn't my type."

"Excuse me, girls," said Mrs. Hunter, interrupting the girls' conversation. "Would you like to tell the class what you all are talking about?"

"No, Mrs. Hunter," said Ayla and Gabriell sadly. They didn't like their teacher at all.

"Be quiet then," Mrs. Hunter said, hating to be interrupted from teaching class.

Ayla and Gabriell nodded their heads. Mrs. Hunter went up to the chalkboard and continued the lesson. The lesson Mrs. Hunter was teaching to her class was biology, Ayla's favorite subject, sarcastically speaking that is.

Ayla was mad at her teacher. She was not interested in listening to the lesson. Bored with class, she decided to stare at her pencil on her desk, hoping the bell would ring for class to end any minute since she was sick of school and boys like Ralph staring at her all the time. Her friend also hoped that the class would end soon.

While Ayla was staring at her pencil, she noticed that it moved all of sudden. It was as if something had touched it, but nothing had.

Ayla thought her eyes or her imagination were playing tricks on her, but then her pencil moved again. She couldn't believe what was happening. It was as if she was in a movie, starring as Superwoman. This wasn't a movie though. This was real! Realizing what she had done, she stared at the pencil again to make sure it was really her making the pencil move and not something else, like the force of gravity or the wind. She made sure her mind stayed focused on the pencil and not anything else, hoping she was really doing it by herself. As she stared at the pencil once more, it moved even more than it had did before. Now she knew that she did it!

That's amazing! Ayla thought as she looked at the pencil. She couldn't believe that she had actually made the pencil move.

What a neat power! *Ayla thought.* I feel like I am a hero in a movie! I wonder how this happened though? Could it have something to do with the spaceship my friends and I were in last night?

Ayla wondered about the power she now had while she waited for class to end. *What all can my mind move? Could it even move a car or a person?* Ayla pondered those questions and many more about her new power that she had just discovered. While those questions were going through her mind, the bell rang for class to end. She heard the bell and ran out of the classroom.

Ayla didn't waste any time getting out of class. She couldn't wait to show her friends what she had discovered—a power she didn't think was possible in the real world, a power she thought was only possible in movies and fairy tales.

Ayla ran into Erica, Mike, and Glenn at her locker. Gabriell was nowhere to be found. Ayla had completely forgotten to tell her in class, and she hated that. But Mrs. Hunter would have probably stopped her from telling Gabriell about her power, anyway.

"Guess what?" Ayla asked her friends, thrilled. "I have a secret power."

"What do you mean?" Erica asked Ayla, puzzled.

"Watch Mike's book and you will see what I am talking about," said Ayla as she stared at a book Mike was holding.

"It moved!" said Glenn, surprised and shocked at the same time.

"How did you do that?" Mike questioned Ayla, also surprised.

"I can move objects with my mind," Ayla said, trying to explain her newfound power to her friends. "All I have to do is stare at an object, and it moves."

"Cool!" said Erica, fascinated by Ayla's secret power. "When did you discover this power of yours?"

"In class," answered Ayla.

"Do you think it has anything to do with the spaceship and the aliens we saw last night, or should I say giant bugs?" Mike asked Ayla, struck with curiosity.

"I guess it probably does," Ayla said, thinking back to yesterday. "It is the only thing that explains how I got this power."

"Well, no matter how it happened, you need to keep this a secret just between us for now," Glenn said, not sure the whole world should know this yet.

"Okay," said Ayla with a sigh. "Can I least tell Gabriell?"

"Better not," said Glenn, answering her question while thinking about what could happen if everyone found out that Ayla had a secret power. "If the spaceship and those weird bugs are involved in giving you that power, then we may get powers too. We must find out before we can decide to tell everybody this secret or keep it to ourselves. Let's just wait and see what happens."

"Okay, but do you really think we all could have secret powers, thanks to that spaceship and those bugs?" Ayla asked Glenn curiously.

"Yes, we all got bitten by the bugs, didn't we?" said Glenn, trying to prove his point to Ayla.

"Yes, we did," said Mike, agreeing with Glenn.

"The point is that those bugs probably gave each of us secret powers for one reason or another," Glenn said to Ayla. "Erica, Mike, and I just haven't discovered ours yet."

"I sure do hope you all get secret powers too," said Ayla, smiling.

"Me too," said Erica, wondering what her power could be.

Erica and her friends were all thrilled by the idea of getting special powers from the giant bugs. Many questions pondered through their heads as they went to class. Who would discover their power next? Did the bugs mean to bit them and give each of them special powers? Was this meant to be or just a coincidence? Only the future can answer these questions for Ayla, Mike, Glenn, and Erica.

CHAPTER VI

Glenn was in physical education. He and his friends were playing basketball together. Mike was in physical education too. Glenn loved the sport and hoped to be in the junior varsity team that year.

Mike and Glenn were playing a small basketball game with their buddies. The score was forty to forty-four. Mike and Glenn were on the same team. They were winning!

Mike had the ball. He passed the ball to a friend. His friend caught it and tried to pass the ball to Glenn, but the other team was blocking him from passing. He jumped and passed the ball, hoping Glenn would catch it. Glenn reached for the ball and caught it in his hands. He was close enough to the basket in order to score. Glenn aimed for the basket while a friend of his on the other team was blocking him. He dodged his friend and threw the ball at the basket and scored. Mike gave Glenn a high five, and the ball was handed to the other team. Mike and Glenn's team ended up losing seventy to seventy-three.

After the game, Mike and Glenn went to the boys' locker room to change clothes and take a shower. Their friends ran ahead of them into the locker room. While they were going, Mike threw the basketball to Glenn. Glenn went to catch the ball and missed. Instead of the ball falling to the floor, it bounced off Glenn's arm and landed back in Mike's hand!

Mike was stunned. He couldn't believe that the ball landed right back in his hand. It was like he had thrown a boomerang, but better.

"How did you do that?" Mike asked Glenn, puzzled.

"I don't know," said Glenn, confused.

"See if the ball will bounce of my arm again," Glenn told Mike as an idea popped into his head.

"Okay," said Mike as he threw the ball back to Glenn. Again, the ball bounced off Glenn's arm.

"Hmmm," said Glenn, thinking. "Could this be my special power? My body a shield? Objects bounce off of it, maybe even bullets?"

"Too cool," said Mike, fascinated by the idea that these questions were becoming a fact at this very moment.

"I wonder why my power is totally different from Ayla's," said Glenn, puzzled. "I mean, I thought the power would be similar in some way, but it doesn't appear to be."

"I thought that too," said Mike, remembering Ayla's power. "I guess we will find out in the near future."

Mike and Glenn had no clue how right Mike was about their future.

CHAPTER VII

School was over. Mike and Erica were in karate class. They were in Don's Do Jo, learning the secret art of ninjutsu. The room they were in was filled with pictures of karate students that had been in competitions. Some of the students were black belts, and some were beginners. Each of them had the chance of winning the competitions as long as they had confidence in themselves. That was the key to success in karate class. Don Russel, the karate teacher, had taught his students that.

The walls in the karate room were painted yellow and white. In the front of the room was a mirror that covered the whole wall, so the students could watch themselves do moves, which helps them to make sure they learned how to do moves the right way and not the wrong way.

Don was in the front of the room. He was tall and slender. He had a freckle here and there on his face. His eyes were the color of brown, and he had long black hair that was just a little bit below his shoulders. He was also very muscular. Anybody could see his muscles through his clothes. Don was wearing a karate outfit like everybody else in the class. He was a black belt, so he knew how to teach karate pretty well. Most of the girls in his karate class were attracted to him because they thought he was so cute with his beautiful black hair and his lovely brown eyes.

Don was teaching his students a new kick. He was hoping that his students would be able to learn the kick without too much trouble since it was a hard kick to learn and it was especially hard to master.

"Erica, demonstrate the new kick to the class," Don said to Erica, wanting to see if she had been paying attention in class.

Erica was not interested in learning new karate moves. This was very strange for her. She had always listened and watched the teacher carefully, but today, it was as if she was in another world. Don realized this and decided to test her.

When Erica demonstrated the kick to the class, she did the kick like it was nothing, as if she was a black belt, but she was only a red belt! Her teacher was amazed at how fast she had learned the new kick. The new kick, Don had taught the students, was the roundhouse, a very difficult kick to learn that quick and be good at it, especially for a person with a lower-class belt than a black belt.

"How did you learn that kick so quick?" Don questioned his student, very impressed by her and surprised at the same time. "I didn't even think you were paying attention."

"I'm not sure exactly, but thank you," Erica said to her teacher, shocked that she did the kick so well.

While Erica was standing beside Don, an idea clicked in her head. Could this be her secret power, or was it a hidden talent that she hadn't realize before? Only time would give those answers. Until then, she would have to wonder.

"I do feel more confident today than I ever have," Erica said, trying to stop Don from being suspicious of her.

"Well, keep this up and you will be a black belt at ninjutsu before you know it," Don said, still surprised by Erica doing the roundhouse kick so good.

"Thanks," Erica said with a big smile on her face.

"I have just begun to notice that you are doing better than anybody else in class," said Don, a little suspicious but very proud of his student. "Do you have another person at home that has been teaching you, or have you just been practicing a lot lately?"

"I have been practicing," said Erica, trying to act convincing.

"Well, maybe that explains why you have done so good in class today," said Don, trying to understand how she had learned how to do the roundhouse so quickly.

"Why don't you assist me tomorrow and help me teach the class?" Don said, seeing that his time of teaching karate was almost up for today.

"Really?" said Erica, thrilled with the idea.

"Sure," said Don, wanting to see how good she had really gotten. "Now go on home with the others and don't forget that you have a real talent."

"I won't," said Erica as she left the karate school with the other kids.

Mike and Erica decided to walk home together. Their houses weren't far from the karate school, so they didn't have to drive home. While they were walking, Mike wondered if Erica had just discovered her secret power.

"Do you think that you becoming a pro so quickly today in karate class is your special power?" Mike asked Erica, curious.

"Yes, that idea happened to pop in my head when I was talking to Don in class," said Erica, thinking about it. "What about you though? Have you discovered your power yet?"

"No, but I think we are about to find out," said Mike, noticing that there was somebody behind them.

"What?" said Erica, worried.

"The bullies from school are behind us!" exclaimed Mike, scared. "Let's get out of here!"

"I can take them," Erica said, wanting to make her new secret power useful.

"No, it's too risky," Mike said to Erica, being cautious.

"Ah, come on," said Erica, protesting.

"No, let's go!" said Mike as he grabbed Erica's hand.

They ran as fast as they could toward their houses, hoping the bullies would lose them. It was their only hope of getting home safely.

The bullies who were chasing Erica and Mike were hot on their tail. Their names were Brian Escobach, his brother Jason, and their friend Casey Malone. They loved to pick on people, especially Mike and Erica.

Brain and Jason had messy black hair. Casey had ragged brown hair. Casey and Jason had gold earrings in their left ears. They were all dressed in camouflage. Each of them were at least two hundred pounds; most of it was muscle.

All of sudden, for no unknown reason, Mike stopped running.

"Why did you stop running?" Erica asked Mike as she tried to catch her breath. "They are almost here!"

"I know, but I think I have just discovered my new power," Mike said, thinking about his power, hoping he was right about what he thought his secret power was.

"Well, use it then before we get pancaked by those guys!" exclaimed Erica, anxious to get away from the bullies.

"I will. Just let me carry you!" exclaimed Mike to Erica.

"Huh, I'm not a baby," said Erica, puzzled at Mike's request.

"Come on!" exclaimed Mike to Erica, ready to run so they wouldn't have to deal with the bullies. "This is the only way to get away from those bullies. You will understand everything as soon as we get away from them. You can trust me! Just let me carry you, please!"

"Well, if you put it that way," said Erica as she let Mike pick her up, not sure of what Mike was going to do next. "Whatever you are planning to do better work because the bullies are almost touching us!"

"Just hold on tight," said Mike to Erica, hoping his idea about his new secret power was right because if it wasn't, they were going to be pancaked for sure, maybe even flatter.

Mike started running. The longer he ran, the faster he went. It was like a continuous sprint of energy was running though his body, making him run faster and faster like a bullet in midair. In a matter of seconds, the bullies were gone.

Before Erica and Mike knew it, they had reached Erica's house safe and sound. They were glad to be away from the bullies.

"That was awesome!" exclaimed Erica to Mike, thrilled that his secret power had saved them.

"Thanks," said Mike, happy to discover his special power.

"Now that we have each discovered our secret powers, do you think we will ever use them to save someone?" Mike asked Erica, wondering if it was possible.

"I don't know," said Erica, thinking while looking at Mike. "I never thought of it that way. I hope we get to though. Then we could become heroes and maybe even get famous! We could be called by a great name that is for heroes with special powers only."

"Okay," said Mike, thinking of all the names they could be called. "How about the Super Teenagers?"

"That doesn't sound right," said Erica, thinking about her being a hero. "What about the Special Ones?"

"That is a good title for us," said Mike, agreeing with Erica.

"We shall be called the Special Ones!" said Erica, happy with the title for them. She hoped that Glenn and Ayla would like the name too.

"Well, we got our special name, but what about those aliens, those giant moths from outer space?" Mike said, thinking back to last night when he and his friends saw the spaceship with strange aliens in it. "Do you really think they did this to us? Do you really think they could have done it for a good reason if they did?"

"I don't know if they did this to us or not," said Erica, not sure. "It does fit all the pieces into the puzzle though, but it sounds too much like a fairy tale."

"Yes, but this one is real," Mike pointed out to Erica.

"I guess you are right," Erica said to Mike, thinking. "We will just have to wait until the future to see if those aliens really did start all this."

With those last few words, Erica waved goodbye to Mike and went into her house. Mike went home too. Mike hoped that those newfound powers would help them to become heroes in the near future.

CHAPTER VIII

That night, Gabriell and her best friend, Courtney Gant, was working on a science experiment with some chemicals. Gabriell loved science and always wanted to be a famous professor when she grows up, just like her father. Courtney, on the other hand, just liked to assist her friend and have some fun at the same time.

Courtney had brown hair just like her friend, but not as long. She had brown eyes and a slightly pointed nose. Courtney was a kind girl that loved to help her friends in any way she could. Courtney and Gabriell had been best friends since the first grade. They knew each other by heart and hope to be best friends forever.

Courtney and Gabriell were working in Gabriell's very own lab, next to her room. They were working at a big table on the right side of the room in the corner. Shelves filled with chemicals and books covered the room. The walls were teal. Gabriell loved the room very much. She enjoyed doing experiments in it all the time. It was her hobby and her hidden talent. She hoped to enlarge the room one day so she would have more room to work with her concoctions. Until then, she would do what she could with the space she had.

Courtney and Gabriell were working on an experiment they called Power. It was supposed to boost a person's energy and make them twice as strong as they were. Courtney and Gabriell were testing it on mice, hoping their formula would be a success.

Gabriell and Courtney were alone in Gabriell's house. Gabriell's parents had went out to eat by themselves. It was their anniversary. Ten years of being a happy couple. They plan to be back home in two hours. Gabriell was their only child.

It was ten thirty at night. Gabriell was glad to have her friend overnight to keep her company. Outside the moon was full, and the stars were bright. There was a stranger in the distance. This person was slowly creeping toward Gabriell's home.

The stranger was a man. He was a tall, slender man with black eyes and big ears that stuck out from his short curly black hair. The man was also very muscular. He was wearing dark clothes to camouflage himself. The man wanted nobody to see him for he was about to break into a house, and that house happened to be Gabriell's. He was ready for some action.

Gabriell's house was a brick house with black shingles on the roof. It was a nice one-story home. The man looked at the house. He was trying to see if he was at the right house. He made sure by looking at the house very carefully. He could see two windows from the front of the house. There was probably more windows at the back of the house. He couldn't see through the windows because the lights were off in the rooms. There was also a wooden door at the front of the house, with a porch attached to it. The porch had two white chairs beside the door and a bench swing in the right corner of the porch. Seeing that the house fixed the description that he had pictured, he smiled. Glad that he was at the right place, he looked around for a way in, hoping no one would hear him.

The man wanted to steal an experiment from the house. He had heard rumors that a girl lived there who was working on a potion to give people more energy. He wanted to see if the rumors were true because he needed the experiment to help him with his evil plans to control Walt Town, the town that Gabriell and Courtney had lived in all their life.

Gabriell and Courtney had no idea that somebody was coming into Gabriell's home. They were working hard on Gabriell's experiment. They were discovering that it was becoming a success as they saw a mouse run up a wheel faster than they had ever seen before. The potion was certainly giving the mouse plenty of energy to run up the wheel. Gabriell and Courtney were glad that the formula was finally working because they had tried it many times before and it had happened to be a failure.

Meanwhile, the stranger had found his way into Gabriell's house by an unlocked window. He crept slowly through the window and into the house. He walked very quietly toward the noise of Gabriell and Courtney talking in the distance. All he could hear was whispering, but it was enough for him to easily find where the two girls were in the house. He passed through the kitchen. He walked very cautiously across the wooden floor. He tried his best to not make any noise that would make Courtney and Gabriell come out of the lab.

As he walked through the kitchen, he saw that it was filled with cabinets full of glasses, bowls, silverware, and other things needed to make food and beverages. There was a big dining table in the middle of the room. A refrigerator stood next to some cabinets on the right wall. There was also a kitchen sink filled with dishes. It was next to some cabinets on the left wall. The walls were painted off-white, and a wallpaper border filled the top of the walls. The border was of many different kinds of flowers. It made people feel like they were outside, cooking. The man didn't like the kitchen at all. He thought it was too pretty and elegant.

After he had walked through the kitchen, he came to the den. It was filled with furniture and pictures. There was a television in the left corner of the room. It was on, even though nobody was there to watch it. Gabriell and Courtney apparently had left it on by accident. It was showing the news. Furniture surrounded the television, from couches to armchairs. The furniture was very comfortable. Anyone could easily fall asleep on them. The walls were painted dark green and covered with pictures, some of family members and some of historical landmarks. The stranger didn't care too much for the den either as he walked through it.

Now the stranger had reached the hallway. He was very close to the lab now. It was at the end of the hallway. He could hear the voices of the girls good. He crept very quietly across the carpet into the hallway. The man was still being very cautious to not make a sound. The walls in the hallway were beige. They were filled with quilts and shelves. The quilts were handmade. They were filled with many different colors, from red to solid black. They were of shapes in patterns. Each of the quilts were very pretty and unique. Even the stranger liked them a little bit.

The man was then at the door of the lab. He carefully peeked through a window that was on the door. He saw that Gabriell and Courtney were focused on their work. He watched them realized that the experiment was a success by seeing the mouse run up the wheel like lightning. A big evil grin covered his face as he watched the two girls. He was so glad that the rumor was true.

As the man looked through the window at the girls, he thought about what he was going to do. I will get the formula and take the kids too. They could show me how to make the energy, the power I need to rule this town I am in and eventually the world! They could be good for ransom too. Too bad they don't have a clue at what is about to happen to them. They will know and see soon enough though. I am going to enjoy this, *the man thought as he carefully turned the doorknob to the lab. The door slowly moved as he turned the knob. He didn't make a sound. Before he knew it, he was in the lab.*

Gabriell and Courtney were thrilled that the experiment worked. They had no idea that somebody was behind them at that very moment, watching their every movement, even their breathing.

The stranger knew that he now had the chance to grab Courtney and Gabriell while their attention was on themselves. The only noise was the rolling of the mouse wheel. The stranger quietly walked toward his victims. He crept closer and closer to them. His footsteps vibrated very quietly across the wooden floor. Gabriell and Courtney still did not notice that somebody was about to grab them.

Once the stranger was close enough to his victims, he slowly edged his arms and hands toward their heads. Then the man quickly moved his hands over their mouths. The girls struggled with all their might as they tried to get away from the man. The man didn't have much of a problem holding on to the girls because he was very strong. He had been lifting weights for many years. But just to make sure the girls didn't try anything, the man spoke to them in a loud, deep voice.

"I have a gun. Try anything and I will shoot. Understand?" The girls nodded their heads. They were very frightened by the man.

The man took his hands off the girls and told them to get Gabriell's experiment off the table. He motioned with his gun in his hand. They hesitated for a moment.

"Do it!" the man yelled. He was getting impatient with them.

Gabriell picked up a flask that had her formula in it. She looked at her experiment and realized what the man could do with it.

"I will not give you our lifework!" Gabriell said to the man. "You will use it for evil purposes. I refuse for that to happen. It is for the good. Not the bad, like you!"

"Okay, tough girl," said the man, getting frustrated with Gabriell, "how about this, either you give me the potion, or you and your friend die?"

"Okay, here," said Gabriell sadly as she handed the man her experiment in a flask.

Gabriell couldn't believe what was happening. She had worked so hard on this concoction of hers that would help people do their job at work. Now she felt like all her work was for nothing because this evil man had her experiment now. Gabriell was sure that the man would use it for evil and not good because it was written all over his face. The way the man had been acting around her and Courtney had let Gabriell know that the man didn't care about them. He just wanted Gabriell's experiment all to himself!

The man looked at Gabriell's potion in his hand. It was in a small clear flask. He could see that it was yellow-green. The man looked at it carefully. He was trying to decide if he should taste it to see if it worked on humans and not just mice, or any animal for that matter. After a minute had passed, he finally decided to taste Gabriell's experiment. He slowly poured it into his mouth and swallowed.

Gabriell and Courtney silently watched the man taste the substance. They wanted to get away from the stranger. They wished and hoped Gabriell's parents would get home any minute, even though they knew that Gabriell's parents wouldn't be home for another hour. Gabriell and Courtney were terrified. They were afraid that the formula would not work on the man because they did not have a chance to test Gabriell's experiment on people. They were afraid he would lose his temper and hurt them or maybe even kill them because it wasn't powerful enough to give people more energy. At least not yet anyhow. At least that was what Gabriell and Courtney thought until they saw the smile on the man's face.

The man felt the experiment working inside his body. He could feel the energy inside him. It was growing. He was becoming very strong and powerful as more and more time passed. The potion had worked perfectly. It was a true success!

"You did a good job, but now that you have seen me, I am afraid that I will have to take you to my home. Then I will kill you and your friend once you have made me more of this," the man said to whom he thought was Gabriell.

"Isn't there any other way?" said Courtney, scared.

"Afraid not," said the man as he smiled an evil smile.

"Now follow me," the man said as he motioned with his gun toward the door of the lab.

Courtney and Gabriell followed the man. They were scared and worried about what was going to happen to them now that this man was kidnapping them. They wished there was some way to get away from the man without getting hurt. All they could do was hope that somebody somewhere would help them somehow, but they knew no one could help them now, for they were all alone with the man and his gun.

CHAPTER IX

"Nooo!" screamed Ayla as she woke up from a horrible nightmare. Then Ayla realized that she was safe in her own room. Ayla looked at her clock beside her bed on her vanity. It showed eleven o'clock at night. She had only been asleep forty-five minutes.

Was it really just a dream? Ayla thought and questioned herself while she was looking at her clock. "It seemed so real. It couldn't have been just a dream. Could it?"

Ayla had dreamed that Gabriell and Courtney were in some kind of danger. In her dream, she saw Gabriell, Courtney, a man, and a gun in the man's hand. She could barely see them. They appeared to be in a room in Gabriell's house, but the dream was so vague that Ayla couldn't tell where they were in the house.

The dreamed scared Ayla. She knew that Gabriell and Courtney were alone at Gabriell's house. Knowing that, she decided to call Gabriell just to be on the safe side.

Meanwhile, the man in Gabriell's home had forced Gabriell and Courtney out of the house and into his truck. His truck was dark brown. It was an old Ford truck covered with mud. Gabriell could barely tell it was a Ford. It was a two-door truck with no air conditioner. The air conditioner was torn up because mud had got caught in it. On the back of the Ford, Courtney could see the license plate. Surprisingly, she could see the serial code on the license plate and where the truck was from. The truck happened to be from Illinois, the state Gabriell and Courtney were in.

"Get in the car!" the man yelled to Gabriell and Courtney while still holding the gun and Gabriell's experiment in his hand. He was ready to leave. He wanted to get away from Gabriell's house before her folks came home.

As Gabriell and Courtney got into the man's car, it started to rain. The man wasn't bothered by the rain as he cranked up the car and got on the highway. As a matter of fact, it appeared that he loved the rain. The man thought it gave him a smell of danger, of adventure in the air. On the other hand, Gabriell and Courtney didn't care for the rain, especially Courtney. She didn't like the rain because the land would become muggy after a good pour.

Gabriell watched her house go away in the distance. She knew she was going to miss it. Unfortunately, Gabriell knew that she may never see it again, thanks to the man who kidnapped her and Courtney. Nevertheless, Gabriell hoped and prayed that she would see her home and family again one day. Then Gabriell realized that there was a chance to escape from the man: her cellular phone. She had it in her shirt pocket. Thank goodness the man hadn't checked her and Courtney's clothes before they had left Gabriell's house. Now Courtney and Gabriell could have a chance to escape by getting somebody from the outside to help them. All Gabriell had to do was wait for the man to leave her and Courtney alone for a minute so she could call for help, but when would she get the chance?

"Beep, beep, beep!" ringed the cellular phone in Gabriell's shirt pocket.

"What's that informal racket?" yelled the man as he stopped the car in fury.

The man wanted to get to his house and find out how to make that experiment of Gabriell's. He didn't want to waste any time. Somebody could be following him or searching for him because he had the girls. He didn't want anybody to find him or know about him until he knew how to make the potion. The man was so confident that he would be invincible by then. He couldn't wait to see how good the formula would work once it was put to the test!

"It's my phone," said Gabriell, scared and happy at the same time. She was glad that somebody was calling her so she could get help, but then at that very moment, she realized that there was no way she would get the chance to tell whoever was calling that she and Courtney needed help since the man grabbed the phone as soon as he had realized where the noise was coming from. He jerked it out of Gabriell's hand and told them to keep quiet while he answered the phone or they would suffer.

"Hello," said the man as he answered the phone while Gabriell and Courtney watched quietly. They wondered who was on the other line and if that person could help them.

"Is Gabriell there?" Ayla asked the voice on the other line of the phone.

The man paused and thought a minute of a lie he could tell the girl. A lie she would believe so the girl would leave him, Gabriell, and Courtney alone.

"Gabriell, uh, no," said the man, still trying to come up with a good explanation.

"I think she is sleeping with her friend," said the man, trying to act sincere.

Courtney and Gabriell wanted to scream and holler so Ayla could hear them, but they knew that they must not because of the man and his gun in his hand.

"Okay," said Ayla, not sure she believed the man on the other line. She didn't recognize the man's voice. That worried her very much. She thought she knew everybody in Gabriell's family.

Wait a minute, *Ayla thought*. What am I worried about? Gabriell and Courtney are just fine. It was probably just a relative of theirs that I haven't met yet.

"Thank you and goodbye," said Ayla as she began to hang up the phone.

"Goodbye," said the man with an evil smirk. Then the man cut the phone off and threw it out the window. Gabriell's and Courtney's chance to be rescued had just flown out the window, or had it? Ayla had talked to the man. She might could be the hope Gabriell and Courtney were looking for. Would Ayla be suspicious about the man's voice on the phone? Gabriell and Courtney hoped she would so there would be hope for them.

Back at Ayla's house, Ayla was lying in her bed, thinking about her dream and the strange man that had answered Gabriell's cell phone.

"I wonder who that man was that answered Gabriell's cell phone?" Ayla questioned herself. "Was he telling the truth about Gabriell and Courtney being asleep, or was he the man that she saw vaguely in her dream?"

She tried to ignore the horrible thoughts and questions in her mind as she tried to go back to sleep. Ayla hoped and prayed that what she had dreamed was really just a nightmare and nothing more, but she feared that she was wrong.

Meanwhile, Gabriell and Courtney were still in the truck with the man. It was one o'clock in the morning. Gabriell and Courtney were very tired, but they could not sleep until they were safe and far away from the man in the truck. Rain was still pouring down outside the truck. A thunderstorm was brewing. Gabriell and Courtney grew more frightened of the man as they started to hear the rumble of thunder and see the flashes of lightning in the distance. The wind had begun to blow hard. It was howling like a wolf. Gabriell and Courtney tried to stay calm as they went through the thunderstorm. They both hoped that they would get away from the man and through the thunderstorm safe and sound.

Finally, after being another hour on the road, the truck stopped at an old wooden house with a black roof. Gabriell and Courtney could see the whole house good from where they were sitting in the man's truck because there were outside lights shining on the house.

The house was the man's home. It was a scary two-story house with four windows and a door. The house was also surrounded by a mist of fog that was slowly moving around the whole house. The fog gave the house a creepy and frightening look. There were two windows at the bottom part of the house and two windows at the top part of the house. Half of the windows were cracked by a bullet, rock, or something that had hit it. There was not a speck of grass or flowers surrounding the house, only dirt and cement. The house looked like a haunted house that people would go to on Halloween, especially with the wind still howling in the distance. The house frightened the girls as they looked at it from inside the truck.

"Do you like my house?" the man asked the girls as they looked at his home.

"No," said Gabriell. The house gave her the jitters, and this was only from the outside. That's what really scared Gabriell.

"Is it haunted?" Courtney asked the man, frightened and scared.

"No, but it will be soon," said the man as he looked at Courtney's pale face and began to laugh an evil laugh.

"What do you mean?"

"You will see soon enough," said the man while looking Courtney straight in the eye.

Courtney scooted over to the side of the door. She was trying to stay as far away as she could from the evil man. The man watched Courtney and Gabriell carefully as he began to get out of his car and pull back his seat to let Gabriell and Courtney out.

"Get out and don't try anything or else!" replied the man as he told Gabriell and Courtney to get out of the truck.

Gabriell and Courtney followed his orders while wishing there was a way to get out of the mess they were in.

"Follow me into the house," the man ordered the girls. "If you don't obey me, you will suffer!"

The girls nodded their heads and followed the man into the house. As they were forced into the house, they passed by two guards with guns in their hands. They knew now that there was no chance of escaping without dying. An outsider was their only hope now as they slowly ventured into the house.

Gabriell and Courtney passed the den and weapon room as they followed the man. The boards on the floor creaked as they walked through the rooms. The walls were mostly dark colors, like brown, gray, and black. There were no decorations or furniture to be seen anywhere in the house. They began to see more men and women with guns as they came to the hallway that was connected to some stairs that went straight up. The man climbed up the stairs, and the girls were forced to follow him from behind. Once they had reached the top of the stairs, the man told two of his fellow men to take the girls to their room on the right and lock them up in it. The men followed their master's orders.

The men were dressed in army suits from head to toe. They had guns in their hands, and evil lurked on both their faces. One had light-yellow hair, and the other had brown hair. Their eyes were dark blue, and they had tattoos all over their arms. The tattoos were green, yellow, and black. They were of skeletons, hearts, and some weird symbols that Gabriell and Courtney had never seen before. They had no clue of what the symbols meant.

One of the men was missing some teeth. It was not a pretty sight when the man smiled or laughed. The other man had huge eyes that looked like they would pop out any minute. The men frightened Gabriell and Courtney. They didn't like the looks of them one bit.

The men led the girls to their room. Once they had reached the door of the room, they pushed Gabriell and Courtney inside and locked the door behind them. Then they stood beside the door, guarding anyone from going or coming out of the room.

The room was almost pitched dark. Gabriell and Courtney could barely see the whole room. There was no light to be found in the room, except for one lamp in the corner that was standing on top of a chest of drawers next to a bed. The light in the lamp was dim because the light bulb in it was about dead. Gabriell and Courtney didn't like being without hardly no light. Now they truly hoped that the man wasn't lying about the house not being haunted, at least not right now.

Gabriell and Courtney saw that there was only one window in the room. Unfortunately, they were too high up to use the window to escape. Gabriell and Courtney could still hear the howling of the wind through the window, but the thunderstorm was finally ending. They were relieved.

The walls surrounding Gabriell and Courtney were black and brown. Nothing covered the walls, except the paint. There was not even one picture to be found on the wall. The carpet was beige. A bed was in the center of the room. It had off-white sheets on it and black pillows. Courtney and Gabriell walked over to the bed and lay on it.

"What do we do now?" Courtney asked Gabriell while wishing they were both safe at their homes.

"I guess there is nothing we can do now since the only practical way out of this room is the door and it's locked tighter than a drum," said

Gabriell sadly. "We might as well try to get some sleep. Tomorrow will probably be a long day for both us. We probably need to save our strength for tomorrow because who knows what that man is preparing for us in the morning."

"Yeah, I guess you're right. Good night."

"Good night, Courtney," said Gabriell to her friend while praying that help was coming and that this place wouldn't be their home forever.

CHAPTER X

It was morning. Ayla was at school. She was searching hard for Gabriell and Courtney. Ayla was still a little worried about them. She could not get the horrible nightmare about them out of her mind. She soon began to realize that Gabriell and Courtney were not in the school. Ayla was beginning to wonder if her dream was not just a dream after all and that it was a vision instead. She decided to find some of her other friends and ask them if they had heard from Gabriell and Courtney.

Ayla spotted Mike, Erica, and Glenn as she was walking through a hallway filled with lockers. She ran over to them. She hoped that they would be able to help her.

"Have you all heard from Gabriell and Courtney?" Ayla asked them while praying that they knew where they were.

"No, but I did dream a scary dream about them," said Erica, answering Ayla's question while thinking about the dream.

"Did it have anything thing to do with Gabriell and Courtney being with a man that had a gun?" Ayla asked Erica curiously. She wondered if their dreams were similar in anyway.

"Yes, it did!" said Erica, surprised that Ayla knew about her dream. "Are you saying that you dreamed the same dream I did?"

"Yes, I guess I am," said Ayla, realizing that they were getting somewhere. "This must mean that Gabriell and Courtney are really in danger!"

"What should we do now?" Glenn questioned Ayla and his other friends. "Can we save them with our special powers if they really are in danger?"

"I don't know, but we must work as a team in order to find out what really happened to them," said Mike, thinking. "Let's start by going to Gabriell's house for clues. If Gabriell and Courtney are really in danger, Gabriell's parents will know."

"That's a great idea!" said Ayla, pleased with Mike's plan. "Let's cut school and find out what happened to Gabriell and Courtney."

"Cut school?" Glenn questioned Ayla. He was worried about his studies. He was always serious when it came to school.

"They could be in real danger," said Ayla, worried about Courtney and Gabriell. "We must find out what's going on before something really bad happens. The nightmare I had seemed too real to not do something about it. We must do this for them."

"Okay," said Glenn, realizing that Ayla was concerned about her friends. "Let's go!"

With those words, Ayla, Glenn, Mike, and Erica were off to Gabriell's house. They knew Courtney was with Gabriell in her lab last night.

They also knew that Courtney was helping Gabriell do some kind of experiment, but that wasn't enough to help them find out what happened to them, so they went to Gabriell's parents for help. They went over to Gabriell's house in Mike's car. They hoped that all their questions would be answered once they were at her house.

Meanwhile, Gabriell and Courtney were still locked up in a room of the scary old wooden house. They were able to get a little bit of sleep during the night. They didn't get much sleep though. The weather was clear, but the world outside was filled with fog. It surrounded the wooden house all the way around. This gave Gabriell and Courtney a little chill. They were afraid of their future in the house with black and brown walls. Their fear was starting to get to them.

"How are we going to get out of here?" Courtney asked Gabriell, wondering if they were ever going to get out of this horrible place that was swarming with monstrous people with guns.

"I don't know, but at least we know why we are here," Gabriell said to her friend, trying to answer Courtney's question the best she could.

"I guess, but did he have to take us way out here just to get that potion from you?" Courtney asked Gabriell, puzzled.

"He is determined to keep it all to himself," said Gabriell, looking sadly at Courtney. I am not sure if anybody will find us now. This was all my doing. I just wanted to help people, especially old people who don't have much energy to start with. I never thought somebody would use it for evil purposes."

"It's not your fault," said Courtney, trying to cheer her best friend up. "You're a scientist. Your dad is a scientist. It's your job. It revolves around your whole life."

"I know," said Gabriell, thinking about her life. "It's just that it is my fault that you got stuck in here with me just because you're my best friend and you had to help me with my experiments. I shouldn't have invited you over last night. Then at least you would be safe at home."

"It was my choice. I enjoy helping you. You can't predict what's going to happen. You had no clue that your experiment would get you into a heap of danger."

"A heap is right," said Gabriell with a slight smile. "I just hated that it had to end up this way."

"At least we are together," said Courtney, tapping her friend on the back. "We will get through this. Just stay strong and try to be confident that we will get out of her safe and sound."

"I hope we do escape out of here somehow or that somebody saves us by some miracle," said Gabriell while looking at her friend.

Meanwhile, Mike, Glenn, Erica, and Ayla were finally at Gabriell's house. Gabriell and Courtney were last seen there. Mike and his friends went up to the door of Gabriell's house. Glenn knocked on the door and waited for somebody to answer it.

While Glenn and his friends were waiting for someone to answer the door, they took a moment to look at the surroundings. They were standing on some steps. Behind them was a small yard filled with fresh cut grass and a few flowers here and there. The flowers they could see were mostly dandelions. There was also a couple of trees in the small yard. One was an oak tree, and one was a regular old pine tree. They were both very beautiful, even though it wasn't fall. They saw nothing else in the yard, except for a butterfly standing on one of the flowers and birds tweeting in the trees. Then they heard a noise and turned around to see

Gabriell's mom at the door. Gabriell's mom looked at Glenn and his friends standing at her doorstep. She was wondering if they knew that her daughter and Courtney were missing.

Gabriell's mom was Diana San. She had orange eyes and blonde hair that touched her shoulders. Diana had a great figure. She could have been a model if she wanted to. She was wearing a long dress that went down to her ankles. It was black with white polka dots all over it. She looked sadly at Glenn and his friends.

"Do you know where my daughter might be and her friend?" Diana asked Glenn and his friends.

"No, we were worried about them and wanted see if they were okay," replied Mike. We have a feeling that they are in some kind of danger."

"Yes, I fear they are in great danger because I know they wouldn't run away from home," replied Diana to Mike and his friends, upset that her daughter and her friend were missing. "They are too good of kids to do that. My husband and I think they were kidnapped or something last night. It was the only explanation we could come up with."

"It's okay, Diana," said Ayla, trying to get her to calm down. "We thought something might had happen to them because Erica and I dreamed nightmares about them last night."

"What were the nightmares Erica and you had?" Diana asked Ayla, wondering.

"We dreamed that Gabriell and Courtney were with this man that had a gun," said Ayla, trying to explain. "It was like a vision or something because we could barely see them. Then once I woke up, I decided to call Gabriell and Courtney to see if they were okay. By that time, it was eleven o'clock at night, but I felt like I had to call. I had to find out if they were safe. I called Gabriell's cell phone, and a weird man answered the phone. I never figured out who that man was, but it might had been the man we saw in our dream. I don't know for sure though. It's just a theory. Then when I got to school, I discovered that Gabriell and Courtney were nowhere to be found. So I told my friends about my dream, and that's when I found out that Erica had dreamed the same dream I did. When that happened, we decided to come over here and find out if our dream was not just a dream."

"So you think your dream might had been a vision or something?" said Diana, thinking.

"Yes," said Erica, thinking about the dream.

"Interesting," said Diana, fascinated by the idea of the dream being a vision. "Is there anything you can tell me about the dream or vision that could help us find out what exactly happened to Gabriell and Courtney?"

"Only that the man had a gun in his hand and it seemed like he was forcing Gabriell to get something, but I don't know what it was," said Ayla, thinking hard about the dream. She was trying to picture it in her head. "I woke up before I could find out."

"I wonder what he wanted her to get," Diana replied.

"I don't know," said Ayla, thinking. "Could we come in and search for clues in order to maybe answer that question?"

"Sure," said Diana, happy to let Ayla and her friends inside.

As Ayla and her friends walk into the house, they noticed that it was all neat and clean. Most of the walls were either blue or white. All the luxuries of a home were in the house, including the kitchen sink!

"When did you find out that Gabriell and Courtney had disappeared?" Erica asked Diana, wondering.

"Twelve thirty-five," replied Diana, thinking back to last night when she and her husband came home.

"Do you know of anything that was stolen from your house?" Glenn asked Diana, trying to help his friends find out exactly what happened last night.

"Not that I know of," said Diana, trying to think if she had noticed anything missing around the house. "Do you really think Gabriell and Courtney could have been kidnapped?"

"I am afraid so," said Erica sadly. "It's the only explanation for Ayla's dream and mine."

"Yes, I guess you're right," said Diana, really worried about Courtney and Gabriell now.

"Do you know why they could have been kidnapped?" Mike questioned Diana, trying to figure how to fit all the pieces of the puzzle together.

"I don't know," replied Diana, trying to think of something that Gabriell had that could be important to someone. "Wait a minute!" said Diana as an explanation to the kidnapping popped into her head. "They were working on a potion in Gabriell's lab. Something about giving people more energy so they could get more things done in the time they had each day."

"Oh, yes!" exclaimed Ayla. "I remember now. It was all around school. Gabriell was making the experiment of the century that would give people the energy they needed to work all day and even all night."

"So in other words, the man or woman that kidnapped them wanted the energy all to him or herself?" Erica asked Ayla, making sure she had it right.

"Exactly!" said Ayla, overwhelmed with joy. "I think we have hit the jack pot! Let's go check out the lab for more clues."

Ayla, her friends, and Diana went to Gabriell's lab. They were hoping to find some more clues that would lead toward Gabriell and Courtney's disappearance.

In the lab, Ayla, her friends, and Diana searched hard for the clues they needed in order to find and save Gabriell and Courtney. After they had hunted for a few minutes, Ayla noticed something was missing from the lab. It was Gabriell's experiment, but what puzzled her, her friends, and Diana was that there appeared to be no sign of a struggle anywhere.

"Wait a minute!" said Erica as a clue popped into her head. "I understand now why there was no struggle. If Ayla's and my dream are right, then that means that there couldn't have been a struggle because the man had a gun in his hand. Courtney and Gabriell would never try anything if somebody was holding a gun at them. They would be stupid to do that."

"Exactly," said Glenn. "That has to be the reason why there appears to be no struggle. There isn't a single clue to what has happened to them, I mean, besides Gabriell's experiment being gone."

"Thank goodness there is no sign of a person being shot anywhere in the house or this lab, for that matter," said Diana, relieved that Gabriell and Courtney didn't get hurt, while they were in the house with the man. Now that Erica, her friends, and Diana knew that information, they prayed that Gabriell and Courtney were safe wherever they were. Erica and her friends began to realize that there was nothing left to be found in the lab, so Erica and her friends left the lab and thanked Diana for their help.

"Don't worry," Ayla said to Diana, trying to comfort her. Ayla saw how much Diana wanted to see her daughter again by looking into her eyes. "They will be found. We will make sure of that."

"I hope so," replied Diana sadly as she thought about her daughter and Courtney. "I guess I will go call Courtney's mom and tell her what we've found. Let me know if you hear or find anything else."

"We will," said Mike to Diana as he and his friends went toward the door of Gabriell's home.

"Goodbye and good luck to you," Diana said as she waved goodbye to them and went toward the phone.

"Thanks," said Mike and his friends as they opened the door and went out of Gabriell's house.

Mike and his friends walked back toward his car. They were not sure of where to go next. They didn't even know that the answers to their questions about Gabriell and Courtney were right under their noses.

CHAPTER XI

Ayla, Erica, Mike, and Glenn were standing against Mike's car, trying to figure out where they should go next. Glenn stared at the ground, bored to death. His head was tired of thinking about what they should do.

While Glenn was looking at the ground, he noticed something. It was a small piece of notebook paper lying on the ground. He picked it up and read it. Realizing it could be a clue, he got his friends' attention.

"Hey, you guys!" said Glenn happily. "I think I have found something!"

"What is it?" said Erica, anxious to know what he had found.

"I found a note somebody dropped," Glenn replied, excited. "It's a bunch of serial numbers. My hunch is that it is a license plate number to a car."

"Do you think Gabriell or Courtney could have written that note, hoping somebody would find it?" Mike asked his friends while pondering the question in his head. "Do you think this license plate belongs to the man that kidnapped Gabriell and Courtney?"

"You're a genius!" Ayla shouted with glee. "That has to be it. Gabriell or Courtney must had written that note. The handwriting even looks familiar to me. I think it is Gabriell's. Let's go back in the house and tell Diana." Then we can ask to use her phone so we can find out who the license plate belongs to," said Mike, thinking.

"Exactly!" said Ayla. "Let's go!" So they all went back to Gabriell's house to talk to Diana.

Meanwhile, Gabriell and Courtney were still locked up in the room with black walls. They hadn't seen the man who kidnapped them since last night. They hoped to never see him again, but they knew they would. Several questions pondered in their minds while they waited for something to happen to them. Will they find a way to escape from the creepy house? When will the man who kidnapped them come back to see them, and what will he do to them?

Now Ayla and her friends were back in Gabriell's house. Gabriell's mom was still on the phone, chatting to Courtney's mom, Allison. She was so overwhelmed in talking to Allison that she didn't notice them standing beside her.

Ayla and her friends waited patiently for a few minutes. Realizing that Diana was paying no attention to them, Ayla got a piece of paper and a pen out of her jean pocket. Then she started to write a note.

"This is no time to write letters," said Erica with a sense of urgency. "We've got to get Diana's attention without making her mad."

"That's what I am doing," said Ayla, trying to explain. "I am writing her a note that explains to her that we need to use her phone in order to save Gabriell's and Courtney's lives."

"Oh, sorry," said Erica, apologizing. "Please continue."

"No problem! I just hope the clue answers all our questions and leads us straight to Gabriell and Courtney."

"Me too!" said Ayla, agreeing with her friend.

When Ayla was done writing the note, she tapped Diana on the shoulder and handed it to her. Diana read the note. Realizing what it said, she told Allison that Ayla and her friends had a lead and that they needed to use the phone to call the police for help. Allison understood and told Diana goodbye and good luck on finding Courtney and Gabriell.

As soon as Diana had hung up the phone, she asked Ayla and her friends what the lead was.

"We will tell you the info once we get the information we need from the police," Mike replied as he picked up the phone.

"Okay," Diana replied, agreeing with Mike. "I just hope that your lead helps us all to find my daughter and Courtney."

"Don't worry," said Ayla, trying to give Diana some hope that her daughter and Courtney would be okay. "The lead will help us find Gabriell and Courtney. I am almost sure of it."

"I hope you're right because that is the only clue we've got," said Diana while looking at Ayla and her friends.

Mike began to dial the number of the police. Diana and his friends watched him dial. They hoped that this was their chance to save Gabriell and Courtney.

"Hello," greeted a police officer. "This is the police station. What can I do for you?"

"Hi," answered Mike. "Mr. Police Officer, my friends and I need some help."

"Just call me Leo Clamp. What can I do for you and your friends?"

"Mr. Leo, my friends and I know Gabriell San and Courtney Gant from school," Mike said, trying to explain the situation to Leo, "the two kids who turned up missing last night."

"Yes, I heard about them," said the police officer, wondering what his point was. "Do you have some more information about them or something else that we need to know?"

"Yes, sir! We found a piece of paper lying on the ground outside of Gabriell's home that appears to be in her handwriting. On the piece of paper is what my friends and I think is a license plate."

"Okay, read the piece of paper to me," Leo said to Mike.

"ALV743."

"I got it written down," said Leo as he cut his computer on. "I will type it up on my computer and see if it picks up anybody. Give me a few minutes. I will let know when I find something. Do you want to wait or let me call you back as soon as I get something?"

"I will wait. Just be quick," said Mike, hoping this clue they had found was what they had been looking for.

"You've got it," said Leo as he started typing on the computer.

Leo looked through his computer files. License plates covered his screen from top to bottom. He began to search for a match to the license plate Mike had given him. At first, he wasn't successful. But finally after five minutes had passed, he had a match. Then he picked up the phone.

"Hey," said Leo, making sure Mike was still on the other line. "You there?"

"Yes, what did you find?" said Mike, wondering whom the license plate belonged to.

"The license plate belongs to Slash Burns."

"Slash Burns?" Mike said, trying to think if he had ever heard that name before. "I don't know him. What about an address?"

"All I have here is his name and the town he is living in," said Leo, looking at his computer screen. "The town may not be where he is really living at. He could have moved. Who knows?"

"Well, tell us the town then," said Mike, persistent.

"Callington, Illinois."

"Thank you," said Mike, happy that they had something to go by, even though it wasn't very much.

"You're welcome," Leo said, thinking and starting to wonder what the kids were going to do now that they had the information they needed. "But before you hang up, could you answer me one question?"

"Sure, I guess so," said Mike, anxious to get off the phone and get on the road. "What do you want to know?"

"Why exactly did you want this information?" asked Leo, wanting to know everything. "I mean, do you think that your friends got kidnapped or something?"

"Yes!"

Mike briefly explained to Leo about the visions Ayla and Erica had and the experiment of Gabriell that was missing in the lab. He hoped that Leo would grasp the reason why they needed the info so they could try to find Gabriell and Courtney.

"I understand," said Leo, happy with their reasons. "Thanks for your cooperation. I am sorry I got suspicious of you. It's part of my duty as a police officer."

"That's okay," said Mike, smiling on the other line. "We understand."

"I hope you find your friends, but if you get into any kind of danger, please don't hesitate to call us. We will be glad to help. That's what we are here for," said Leo, hoping that Mike was listening.

"Thank you and goodbye, Leo," said Mike as he hung up the phone.

"I have the information we need," Mike told his friends and Diana, happy that they finally had a lead. "The person we are looking for is Slash Burns. He lives somewhere in Callington. Do any of you all know him by any chance?"

"No," said all of Mike's friends and Diana.

"Okay then," said Mike, thinking. "Let's get on the road and head toward Callington."

"I think I better go too," said Diana, wanting to help.

"No, you better stay here and keep us posted if any more leads come up," said Mike. He didn't want Diana to know about their secret powers because he was almost sure that they would have to use them in order to save Gabriell's and Courtney's lives. "We don't have a clue where this Slash is in Callington. If you hear anything about him while we are gone, you can call us on the cell phone. You will help us more that way than coming with us."

"Okay," said Diana, disappointed that she couldn't go with them even though she knew in her mind that it was best. "That sounds good. I will let you know if anything comes up that will help you find my daughter and Courtney."

"Thanks," said Mike and his friends as they headed toward the door.

"We will find them," said Ayla, trying to be confident that they would be able to save Gabriell and Courtney.

"I know you will," said Diana, beginning to have confidence in Mike and his friends. She hoped that she could count on them because they were her only hope. "Good luck. May God be with you."

Mike and his friends walked out of Gabriell's house and went toward his truck. On their way, Glenn wondered who this Slash person really was. Was he a greedy person that wanted Gabriell's experiment, Gabriell, and Courtney all to himself? Did he kidnapped them as part of some kind of plan of his, or did he just do it to get attention?

CHAPTER XII

Gabriell and Courtney were looking for a way out of the room, but they hadn't had any luck. They had checked all the walls and the door a thousand times. They were hoping to find a secret door or something so they could get away from the old wooden house.

"Listen," said Courtney, standing still.

"What is it?" said Gabriell, questioning her friend. "Did you hear a noise or something?"

"Yes, I think someone is coming," said Courtney, swearing she just heard footsteps coming close to them.

"Let's hide," said Gabriell, thinking. "Maybe the person will think we've escaped and go looking for us. Then we could sneak out of this room and try to escape."

"Good idea," said Courtney, excited that they might get a chance to escape. "Let's find a good place to hide."

Courtney and Gabriell quickly searched for a place to hide. Hearing the footsteps come closer, they finally decided to hide under the bed. As they hid under the bed, they didn't seem to notice the chains that were around the bed where other people had been torture and killed. They were too concerned with escaping to notice or worry about getting chained up. The only problem was that the person who was about to come into the room was too smart to be fooled by the girls. The person knew the girls would hide from him because he had kidnapped them.

Once the man reached the door, he unlocked it with a key that he got out of his blue jean pocket. The girls were nowhere in sight, and the man wasn't a bit surprised. The girls watched the man's shoes walk around the room, looking and searching for them. They were scared, but they tried to be as quiet as possible so the person wouldn't find them. The person stopped walking and began to listen. He was searching for a clue to Gabriell and Courtney's whereabouts.

Courtney was really getting scared now. Her heart began to beat fast. She was breathing heavily.

"Relax, Courtney," said Gabriell softly, trying to calm down her friend. "You don't want him to hear us, do you?"

"No, of course not," whispered Courtney. "I just can't help it. I have never been this scared and this much afraid of somebody in my life."

"I know," said Gabriell softly. "We got to be as quiet as possible though. We can't let the man find us."

"Okay. I'll try my best to relax."

The man walked to the bed and sat on it. He knew they could not have escape because the door was locked and he had no hidden doors in the room. He decided to sit on the bed quietly for a few minutes and hope for a clue to pop up. The man was listening for any sound that could help him find Gabriell and Courtney. Then the man thought he heard something. He sat very quietly and listened. Then he heard it again. It was somebody breathing heavily. He then realized that the breathing must be coming from under the bed on his right. He leaned over the bed to his left and saw Gabriell's and Courtney's feet. Seeing that the girls were under the bed, he got off the bed and went down to his knees. The girls had no idea that somebody was about to grab them from behind.

"Where did the man go?" Courtney asked her friend softly, puzzled.

"I don't know," Gabriell whispered, worried.

The man heard the girls talking. He knew he now had the chance to grabbed them while their attention was on each other. They were trying to find him when he was right behind them! Just when the man was about to grab Gabriell and Courtney, he hit a chest of drawers that was right next to him with his arm. The girls heard the noise and turned around to find the man behind them.

"It's you!" Gabriell said, recognizing the man.

"Yes," the man said to Gabriell and Courtney with an evil smile. "I brought you here." Then the man signaled with his gun and said, "Now get out from under the bed. I have something to tell you."

The girls followed the man's orders, realizing they had no choice. They would have been safe by now, but their chance of escaping had just flown away when the evil man found them. Now there was nothing left for them to do but hope for the best. It was all Gabriell and Courtney had now.

"Sit on the bed and hear what I have to say," the man ordered the girls.

Courtney and Gabriell sat on the bed. They were terrified. They hoped that nothing really bad would happen to them. Too bad luck wasn't on their side at the moment.

The man looked at Gabriell and Courtney. He now had on a brown short-sleeve shirt and baggy blue jeans. He had an evil smirk on his face and a cold reflection. Anybody who was brave enough to look at him or stand up to him could see that he was a well-built man who had to be a killer, and he was indeed a true killer. Courtney and Gabriell was beginning to realize that as they watched the man. They knew he was not afraid to kill as they saw his eyes begin to narrow. He gave Gabriell and Courtney a cold look and then began to speak to them.

"Listen to me well," said the man as he looked at the girls carefully. He still didn't know which one of the girls was Gabriell.

"What do you want from us?" Courtney said to the man before he had a chance to say anything more to them.

"I ask the questions!" replied the man with a loud voice. His eyes narrowed even more. They stayed glued on Courtney and Gabriell, making sure they didn't try anything.

"You just listen!" said Slash in a harsh voice, starting to get mad at Gabriell and Courtney. "Now my name is Slash. I have heard that one of you is Gabriell, a scientist and a good one at that. One that knows how to make energy without just food. One that gives people more strength and power to do things. I want to use that power to rule your town and then the world, so tell me which one of you is Gabriell."

Gabriell and Courtney refused to speak. They dared not tell who was who when they had a choice. Gabriell didn't want Slash to use her experiment for his own needs so he could rule the world. Courtney didn't want her best friend to suffer the consequences of knowing how to make the experiment. She knew there was no telling what he would do to her to make her make more of her experiment for himself. They kept their mouths shut, hoping Slash would not force them with his gun to tell which was who and who was which.

"Tell me now," said Slash, getting mad at the girls, as he lifted up his hand and pointed his gun straight at them. "Or I will choose who it is and shoot the other person. Don't think I want because I am a killer. I will kill one of you if I have to."

"Okay, you've won," said Gabriell sadly. Her eyes watched Slash put his gun down, away from the girls, and into his jean pocket. "I am Gabriell," replied Gabriell in a low voice.

"Thank you for your cooperation," Slash said, pleased with himself. "I promise you, you won't regret it. Now that I know who I am talking to, I am pleased to tell you that I have made a decision. It will force you to tell me how to make your experiment, besides saying I will kill you. That's too easy for a killer like me. I need to make your friend and you suffer so I will get something out of it besides your experiment. Since I am a greedy person, I will take everything I can get my hands on."

"No matter what you plan to do to make us suffer, I will never make you my experiment," said Gabriell, hating the idea of Slash using her experiment on himself in order to rule the town they lived in and then the world. "I refuse to give you something you don't own, something you want all for yourself, in this case, my experiment. Well, I got news for you. You are not going to get nothing out of me unless you dig really deep because I am not giving you any more of my experiment without a fight."

"We'll see about that," said Slash, happy to have a challenge. It was no fun for him to get somebody to do something for him without the other person fighting before they finally did what they were told.

"There are some chains under the bed if you didn't notice before. I will latch both your friend and you up under the bed, and to spice things up, I will give your friend and you a potion, or should I say, poison. It is called Deasia. *Dea* for death. Lovely name, isn't it?" The girls didn't answer.

Slash continued, "I think it is. The poison will make your friend and you groan in agony after it has been in both your systems for a while. And don't worry, it won't take the poison long to take effect. Once you both have been tortured enough and you have decided to tell me how to make more energy for myself, I will give your friend and you an antidote. Oh, and another thing. You will only have eleven hours to live after I have forced the potion down your throats. So in other words, if you don't make more energy for myself, your friend and you will be dead before this day is over with. And don't think somebody will save you before you both die because it won't happen. You are both over a hundred miles away from your homes. So if you are waiting for somebody to rescue you, good luck because you both will be dead by the time they find you. Now get back under the bed so I can latch both of you up."

The girls followed Slash's orders. They crawled under the bed, scared to death. They hoped and prayed that there was still a chance of getting out of the sticky situation they were in. Unfortunately, their chance of escaping had just became very slim.

"Now I will latch you up," said Slash, looking down at Courtney and Gabriell under the bed. "Do not struggle or try to get away from me or you will regret it, and that I guarantee." Then Slash started latching the girls to the bed, making sure each latch was tight and secure so they would not escape from him.

"You won't get away with this!" yelled Gabriell, looking hard into Slash's eyes, wishing there was some goodness in him somewhere, but there was none to be found.

"We'll see about that," said Slash, confident that he would get what he wanted from Gabriell.

Once Slash had finished latching up the girls, he got a potion out of his pocket on his brown shirt. The potion was in a flask with a cork to seal it. Half of the flask was filled with the potion. It was the color of gray. It looked disgusting to Gabriell and Courtney. It reminded them of wet clay.

"Like I said before, this potion will make you suffer a long agonizing death of eleven hours," said Slash, trying to explain some things about the poison he was about to give them. "The cure is only known by the person that invented this poison, and that person happens to be me, Slash Burns."

Courtney and Gabriell were scared and afraid. They hated seeing the poison in Slash's hand, knowing that that toxin would soon be in their bodies slowly killing them. They were dreading their future, wishing there was some way to convince Slash that he didn't need to give them the poison in the flask, that the chains were enough, but Slash wanted Gabriell to make more energy for himself, and he wanted to make sure that she would do it. Slash knew that if the chains did not work, the poison would force Gabriell to make the energy for Slash. Surely, she wouldn't lose her life just because of an experiment, or would she? Of course, there was only one way to find out, so he reached down under the bed, ready to force the toxin down Gabriell's and Courtney's throats.

"Now it is time to give you my precious potion," said Slash as he watched Gabriell's and Courtney's faces turn white in fear.

"Isn't the chains enough?" Courtney begged Slash, not wanting to die from the poison.

"No," replied Slash in a harsh voice. "This is the only way for me to take make sure that your friend here will make her potion for me, unless you can convince her otherwise."

"No, you don't deserve her experiment!" said Courtney loudly. "It is her lifework. She should be able to make it for someone that really needs it, like old people that are slowly dying of old age, not evil people like you that don't have a care in the world!"

"That is just tough, isn't it?" Slash remarked at Courtney. "Whether you like it or not, sooner or later, Gabriell will be forced to make the experiment for me."

Then Gabriell butted in. "No matter what that poison does to our bodies, I will never make more of my experiment for you!" yelled Gabriell, trying to convince Slash that she meant business.

"Suit yourself," said Slash to Gabriell, confident that he was going to win, that he was going to get more of the experiment so he could conquer the world. "It is you that will suffer, not me."

The girls paid no attention to what Slash had just said to them. They just lay under the bed and hoped for the best because that was all they could do.

Slash took the cork off the flask. He slowly moved the flask toward Gabriell's and Courtney's mouths. Then he poured the poison down

Gabriell's throat and then down Courtney's throat. They tried not to swallow the liquid, but Slash made sure they did.

"The toxin will take full effect in one hour," said Slash to Gabriell and Courtney. "From then on, you and your friend will suffer until you tell me how to make more energy so I can become powerful and rule the world," said Slash, excitedly expressing his dreams.

"Somebody will save us before we are forced to reveal my experiment to you," said Gabriell, trying to convince Slash that his plans might get blown up. "That person is probably on his or her way right now."

"Sure, when you are already dead and buried," Slash remarked to Gabriell and Courtney while laughing at them. "Your friends and family members are three hours away from here if you both didn't notice. They will never find you by the time I am through with both of you. So don't worry about anybody saving you because it won't happen," Slash added, making sure they understood that there was not a chance of them escaping from him and his old wooden house.

"We'll just see, won't we?" remarked Gabriell back, trying to act courageous. "I will not give up when I know there is a chance of somebody rescuing us, and I know there is," said Gabriell to Slash, trying to get his attention. She wanted to scare Slash bad because of what he had already done to her and Courtney, putting poison down their throats, threatening them, and latching them up.

"You can say all you like, but you are never getting out of here alive!" said Slash, going toward the door of the room. He was very confident that he was going to get everything he wanted very soon. "Oh, and one more thing. Holler when you are ready to make your experiment for me. Ha ha ha!"

"*Never!*" Gabriell yelled as Slash left the room and locked the door behind him.

Slash walked down the stairs with a smile on his face. He was so glad that things were going just as he had planned. He couldn't wait for Gabriell to call his name and tell him that she would make her experiment. He could almost hear her pleading for him to get the chains off her body. The thought bounced in his head, filling his heart with pure evil.

Courtney and Gabriell were latched up as tight as a drum, wishing there was still a way to escape this awful dungeon-like room.

"What are we going to do?" Courtney asked Gabriell, concerned and worried.

"I don't know," said Gabriell, trying to think of a decent answer to her friend's question. "Let's just hope that somebody will find that piece of notebook paper with the license plate on it."

"You're right," said Courtney, starting to cheer up. "Maybe there is a chance of somebody saving us. We just got to hang on until that person gets here. But wait a minute, what if nobody finds the piece of paper?" said Courtney, starting to get worried all over again. "What if somebody doesn't come and save us until we are dead and buried just like Slash had said?"

"We have to think positive," said Gabriell while looking at Courtney. "We must not give up so easily. We can't let Slash get his way."

"I know," said Courtney, thinking. "I just wish we were safe at home in our beds."

"Me too," said Gabriell, wishing the same thing.

The girls tried to hope for the best as they lay under the bed, latched up. They could hear the branches of trees banging against the only window in the room and drops of rain hitting the glass. Another thunderstorm had come to life just like the one the night before. Luck just wasn't on Courtney and Gabriell's side as they waited for their future that was filled with great danger. Their adventure had just begun. The thing they didn't know was that one of them may not survive in the end. Their future awaited.

CHAPTER XIII

Mike, Glenn, Erica, and Ayla were on the road. They were trying to figure out how to get to Callington, the town where Slash Burns lives. Mike was looking at a map for the info they needed to get to the town. Glenn was driving. He was hoping that they were going in the right direction. Ayla and Erica were in the back seat, trying to help Mike find Callington on his map.

"I've found Callington," Mike said, pleased with himself. "We are going in the right direction. The only problem is that Callington seems to be a long way from where we are at."

"How long might that be?" said Glenn, not sure that he wanted to hear the answer to his question.

Mike calculated the distance on his map and then said, "I'm afraid we have a long two-hour-and-half ride until we reach our destination."

"That's almost three whole hours!" exclaimed Ayla, worried about Gabriell and Courtney. "We will be too late to save our friends by then. They will probably be dead by the time we find them."

"We won't be too late," said Erica, trying to convince Ayla that everything was going to be okay. "They're probably just locked up somewhere."

"I hope that they are okay," said Ayla worried.

"We all do," said Mike, joining Erica and Ayla's conversation. Then Mike glanced at his map and told Glenn some directions.

"Stay on this interstate for two hours," Mike said to Glenn while looking at his map. "Then take exit number 87."

"Okay," said Glenn, looking at the road. "Hang on, Gabriell and Courtney. We are on our way."

Glenn and his friends traveled down the interstate, hoping that they would be at Callington soon. They also hoped to find where Slash lives without too much of a problem.

As Glenn and his friends traveled, they had no idea of the dangers that awaited them up ahead. Were they prepared for those dangers? Would their powers be powerful enough to save their friends lives, or would the powers be a failure to them and their friends? Only time would tell.

Courtney and Gabriell struggled to get the latches off. They had no success so far.

"This is hopeless," said Courtney sadly. "We are getting nowhere. All we are doing is wasting our strength."

"I know," said Gabriell, worried about her future in the horrible room. "We must not give up though. That's what he wants."

"Yeah," said Courtney, agreeing with her friend. "At least the thunderstorm is ending, but what are we going to do when the poison takes its full effect on our bodies?" Courtney added, worried and scared.

"We'll just have to deal with it until help comes," said Gabriell, not sure how long they could stand the pain.

"A SWAT team better find us soon, or we will be dead before we know it!" said Courtney, terrified.

Gabriell and Courtney were just beginning their struggle to safety. If they only knew of what was to become of them, they would be prepared for the future. Unfortunately, they didn't, so all they could do was hold on and fight for their survival.

Back on the road, Glenn was still driving on the interstate, hoping they would soon reach their destination in Callington. They had only been on the interstate thirty minutes now. They had an hour and a half yet to go.

The weather was clear. There was not even a cloud in the sky. The sun was shining brightly in the sky. It was two o'clock in the afternoon. The speed limit was fifty-five miles per an hour. The interstate was crowded with cars and trucks of all sizes. They were ahead and behind Mike's car. A truck decided to pass Mike's car. It was white and black. The truck was advertising furniture. The word *furniture* was written in big black bold letters on the middle of the truck.

There was a man driving the truck. He was a chubby old guy who was in his mid-sixties with black eyes and short beige hair. The man also had a small birthmark above his right eye. He was wearing a red nerdy shirt and blue overalls. He was also wearing a cap that had the Braves baseball team on it.

The man driving the furniture truck was not looking where he was going. He swerved on his lane as if he was drunk or something. Glenn tried to get away from him, knowing that the man might hit him and knock him off the road. That could very possibly cause a wreck. Unfortunately, no matter how hard Glenn tried, he could not get away from the truck. The interstate was too crowded with other cars. He was trapped in a pack. Everybody else in Mike's car was asleep. They had no idea of what was about to happen.

The furniture truck swerved once more. This time, it went into the other lane and hit Mike's car. Glenn grabbed the steering wheel and tried to stay on the interstate. When the man hit the car, Erica, Ayla, and Mike woke up from their nap, startled.

"What's going on?" Erica exclaimed, scared and worried.

"I think I am dealing with a drunk driver here," said Glenn, looking at the driver of the furniture truck.

"Hey, man, stay on your lane!" Glenn yelled to the man while finally getting Mike's car back in control, hoping that the man would get some sense into his head.

"You better watch him Glenn," said Mike, being cautious. "There is no telling what he might do if he really is drunk."

Mike didn't want to get into a wreck, especially now when their friends' lives were at stake, whether they knew it or not. Plus, they could get hurt bad themselves if they got into a wreck with the truck, not to mention the other cars that could get involved. There was no telling what was about to happen since they were in a pack. Mike and Glenn knew that the situation they were in was not going to be easy to get out of.

"I know," said Glenn, getting tense.

He knew that his friends' lives were at stake as he firmly grasped the steering wheel. He kept his eyes glued on the road and the driver of the truck.

Unfortunately, the man had ignored Glenn's warning for him to stay on his side of the lane. He swirled again into the other lane. Glenn tried to dodge the truck, but it was too big. The truck hit Mike's car a second time, harder than before. Mike's car swerved out of control. Glenn tried his best to get the car back on his side, gluing his hands to the steering rule and keeping his eyes focused on the road and Mike's car. He swerved into the emergency lane and then finally got Mike's car back in his control. Then he stopped the car and checked to see if everybody was okay. He was relieved that it was all over with.

"Everybody okay?" Glenn asked his friends while catching his breath.

"Yes, we're okay," said Ayla in the back seat, glad that it was all over.

"That was a close one," said Mike while looking at the interstate.

"Too close," said Glenn, trying to get over the ordeal he just went through with the man and his lovely furniture truck.

"Are you okay?" said Mike to Glenn, worried about his friend.

"Yes, I am fine. I just need to catch my breath and try to relax," answered Glenn.

"Okay, I'll drive then," said Mike, trying to get Glenn to calm down.

"Good, because I have had it with driving today," said Glenn while seeing flashes of the man hitting Mike's car going through his mind at that very moment. "I am not sure if I ever want to drive again."

"The highway is a dangerous and scary place, but everybody has to deal with it sooner or later," said Mike, trying to prove a point.

"I know. I just wish it didn't have to happen to us," said Glenn, pondering the thought.

"Don't we all?" said Erica, joining Mike and Glenn's conversation. "Who was that guy, anyway?"

"Some drunk truck driver, I suppose," said Glenn, thinking about the incident that had just occurred.

"That was some driving!" Ayla replied, getting into Mike, Erica, and Glenn's conversation. "You did a good job of handling Mike's car. I just hope the man didn't dent it up too bad."

"Me too," said Mike, getting worried about his car.

"We better go check it out," said Glenn, hoping Mike's car was not scratch up too bad.

Glenn and his friends got out of Mike's car and looked at it. Cars and trucks kept on going past them as if nothing had happened. The supposedly drunk driver in his furniture truck was gone. He was nowhere to be found. They hoped and prayed the man wouldn't cause a serious wreck somewhere up the interstate.

Mike's car was okay, except for his door. It was dent badly and would not open up. Glenn had to get out of the car on the passenger side, although he was tempted to crawl over the door like *The Dukes of Hazzard* boys! The car looked okay compared with what could have happened.

After Mike and his friends had finished inspecting the car, they got back into it. Mike went into the driver's seat, hoping that the drive from here on out would be safe and not dangerous like it had been a few minutes ago. Ayla and Erica were still in the back. Glenn was sitting in the front with Mike. Glenn hoped to never get in a situation with a drunk person ever again. He had quite enough adventure for today. Unfortunately, he had only seen a piece of what's to come for him and his friends.

Meanwhile, the poison in Gabriell's and Courtney's bodies had taken full effect. They were beginning to suffer from the poison. While

Gabriell and Courtney lay under the bed in pain, they hoped and prayed an outsider would come and rescue them.

"Uh," mumbled Gabriell, struggling. "I don't know how much longer we can take this."

"Relax, Gabriell," said Courtney, trying to get Gabriell to calm down. "The poison is barely bothering me, so it can't be bothering you too bad."

"Slash gave you less of the toxin than he gave me," said Gabriell, getting flashbacks of Slash forcing the poison down their throats. "Don't you realize that?"

"I am sorry," said Courtney, apologizing. "I didn't know."

"Well, he did just to force me to make my experiment for him," pointed out Gabriell. "What people will do to get what they want."

"Try not to worry about it," said Courtney while looking at Gabriell. "Just hang tough and hope that help will come soon."

"I'm trying to fight it, but it's not easy," said Gabriell, hating the poison more and more as the minutes passed by. "How long has it been since the poison has been in our bodies?"

"An hour and thirty-five minutes according to my watch," Courtney said. Her watch had a white cat in the center. The paws were the hands of the clock.

"That's all?" said Gabriell, surprised. "It seems like three hours, if not longer. I never thought an hour and a half would last so long."

"No kidding," said Courtney to Gabriell.

The girls continued lying under the bed, suffering from the latches and the poison in their bodies. Was this room where Gabriell and Courtney were going to die? This was certainly not the way they had pictured it.

CHAPTER XIV

Mike, Erica, Ayla, and Glenn were finally off the interstate. They had reached Callington and did not have far to go now. They hoped and prayed that they could find where this so called Slash lives before it was too late to save their friends.

They were very worried about Gabriell and Courtney, especially Ayla. They hoped that their friends were okay and not in serious danger and that they would be able to save them before something bad happens to them. At least they knew why Gabriell and Courtney were kidnapped.

Ayla and her friends had no clue where to go from here on out. They had never been in Callington before, and they had certainly never heard of a guy named Slash. They stopped at a gas station and parked in the parking lot, hoping somebody would know Slash and would be able to give them directions to his house.

The gas station was owned by a family. It was a small brick building. The store was called Stan's Place. Stan was the owner of the store. The walls around the store were painted brown. There were two big windows in the front of the store and two revolving doors. You could see people buying stuff through the windows. It was a popular store. People loved to stop at Stan's to talk with him, buy his fresh foods, and pay for gas. He was a nice and friendly person to be around. He knew a lot of the local townsfolk.

Ayla and her friends looked at the store for a moment and then went in. The store was small inside. There were two aisles of food and frozen foods against the left and right walls of the store. The walls in the store were painted white. Ayla and her friends didn't need any food, so they went up to the salesclerk who was behind a booth and asked him for help on finding where Slash lives. They hoped that the person could help them.

The person standing behind the booth was the owner of the store, Stan Lance. He was standing behind his cash register, looking at Ayla and her friends. He wondered what they wanted since they didn't have food in their hands and didn't buy any gas.

Stan had short brown hair and dark-green eyes. He was a skinny and muscular guy who was in his mid-thirties. He was wearing a wedding ring. Stan also had on a black long-sleeve shirt and baggy blue jeans to match. There was a tag on his black shirt next to his shoulder. The tag had these words written in big bold letters: "Welcome back!" At the very top of the tag was his name. He smiled at Ayla and her friends and asked them what they needed help with.

"Can I help you?" Stan asked Ayla and her friends.

"I hope so," said Mike to Stan, hoping the man could help them find where Slash lives. "Have you heard of a guy named Slash Burns, and do you know where he lives?"

"Yes, I think I have," Stan said, trying to think back to when he had last heard and saw Slash. "He has come to this store before. He is a very strong and ruthless man. I don't think you want to know where he lives. Believe me, he is not a guy you want to mess around with. He doesn't like strangers, and he wants nothing to do with them. Are you sure that you want his address because I am sure that you will regret it in the long run?"

Stan scared Glenn and his friends with the things he told them about Slash, but they knew that they had to find where he lives so they could save Gabriell and Courtney. So Glenn decided to explain their situation to Stan. He understood and gave them Slash's address.

"Okay," said Stan, not sure if he was doing the right thing. "Stay on Highway 9 until you get to a small dirt road on the left called Dark Street. It should be about five miles down Highway 9. Then go down the dirt road for exactly six miles. Once you have drove the six miles, you will come to an old two-story wooden house on your right. That is Slash's home. It has a black roof and four windows on the front of the house. It is the only house not surrounded by grass or shrubbery, so you should be able to spot it easily."

"Thank you," Glenn told Stan, glad that they now knew the way to Slash's home. Now they could finally go and save Courtney and Gabriell, if it wasn't too late already.

"You all be careful now," said Stan, warning Glenn and his friends about Slash. "That place can be very dangerous. If you get in a sticky situation, don't be afraid to call for help."

"Will do," said Glenn to Stan with a smile. "Thanks again!" Then Glenn and his friends left the store and went back into Mike's truck.

Glenn and his friends were pretty sure that they were on the right track. They were so glad to finally know the way to Slash's house. All they had to do now was to be careful and to not get themselves in trouble. Too bad that is easier said than done for them because they have got a very dangerous road ahead of them as soon as they get to Slash's house.

Meanwhile, Slash was in his research lab. He was getting impatient with the poison he gave Gabriell and Courtney. He thought it took too long for the poison to take effect. Slash was ready to become all mighty and powerful. He didn't want to wait any longer to get what he wanted, so he sat down and tried to think of an idea that would speed things up.

"Ah-ha," said Slash as a light bulb clicked in his head, "I have a perfect idea."

Slash got a controller out of the top drawer in his desk. The controller was black. It had lots of buttons on it. The buttons were of all kinds of different colors: red, green, purple, blue, pink, etc. Slash looked at the controller, and then he pressed the red button that was on the left side of the controller in the middle. Then he laughed an evil laugh. Slash was very pleased with himself and the great idea he had thought of. He knew that he had a great advantage over Gabriell and Courtney now. Slash couldn't wait to hear them holler for help because he knew that pressing that button would definitely make one of them, if not both of them, speak up any second now.

The red button will make the restraints around Gabriell and Courtney tighter and tighter until Gabriell is forced to tell Slash how to make more energy. Then he can rule the world! What will Gabriell and Courtney do now?

Back under the bed, Courtney was messing with one of her latches, trying to get loose. She was having no success. Then something horrible began to happen that they least suspected.

"Oh no!" Gabriell said in a low terrifying voice while pleading to her friend. "Help me! The restraints are getting tighter around my whole body. I am losing my circulation. The latch around my neck is choking me. I can't breathe! Please help me!"

"Hang on!" exclaimed Courtney, trying to comfort her friend and fight the latches that were also getting tighter around her body. "I'm here. Just hold on!"

Gabriell's latches were getting tighter and tighter than Courtney's. She was fighting a losing battle. She had no chance over the restraints, and she knew it but was afraid to admit it.

"I can't hang on!" said Gabriell in a low voice, still terrified. She was afraid that she was going to die under the bed.

"Yes, you can," said Courtney, trying to convince Gabriell to hang on while trying to ignore the latches that were getting tighter around her neck. Then Courtney saw the look on Gabriell's face. She realized that it was time to yell for Slash. Either that or watch Gabriell die and she refused to do that.

"I'm going to have to shout for Slash," Courtney told Gabriell. She hoped she was doing the right thing.

"You can't!" mumbled Gabriell while beginning to breathe heavily.

"I must!" exclaimed Courtney, worried about Gabriell. "It's the only way. I can't just watch you die."

"Slash!" Courtney yelled as loud as she could. "We'll tell you how to make more energy. Just help Gabriell!"

"Ah, the sound of help," said Slash with an evil smile. "Just what I needed to hear." Then Slash left his lab and went to the room where Gabriell and Courtney were.

"Did I hear the word *help*?" said Slash, putting his hand against his ear while coming into the room.

"Yes!" exclaimed Courtney to Slash. He was at the bed about to bend under it to see his guests. "Please help Gabriell!"

"If I do save her, will she make me more powerful? Then I can rule your town and conquer the world," Slash questioned Courtney, not even caring that Gabriell was dying at that very moment and that the restraints around Courtney were still getting tighter.

"Yes, she will," said Courtney, scared for her friend. "Just please take off her latches and then mine so you can give us the antidote for the poison you gave us."

"You promise she will?" Slash questioned Courtney while Gabriell was gasping for breath.

"I promise. Just help her now!" exclaimed Courtney, seeing Gabriell dying. Slash must help Gabriell now, or she will die!

Slash went to work, taking the latches off Gabriell. He started with her neck and ended with her feet. Then he took the restraints off Courtney. He made sure that he got all the latches off both of them. Then he tied their hands and legs with a rope so they wouldn't try anything. He knew they were very weak but still didn't want to take any chances. Once he was done, he reached in his pocket of his jacket for the antidote that Gabriell and Courtney needed. It would take the poison out of their bodies. He gave it to Gabriell and waited for it to work. He completely ignored the thought that Courtney needed the antidote too.

"What about me?" said Courtney, wanting the antidote. She was tired of fighting and suffering from the poison that was affecting her body.

"Later," said Slash, wanting to rule their town and the world as soon as he could.

"She won't make the energy for you if you don't give me the antidote too," said Courtney, trying to convince Slash.

"Not if I hold a gun to her face and yours!" exclaimed Slash, pointing out with that evil smile of his.

Courtney nodded her head. She was starting to get really scared for her and Gabriell. Gabriell was very relieved to get the latches off. She almost choked to death because of the restraint around her neck. She had never come so close to death in her life. That really terrified Gabriell, and she didn't like it one bit. Gabriell was glad that she was going to be okay, at least for a while anyway. She was glad that it was over, except for the poison. Thank goodness that was getting taking care of at that very moment. Slash didn't have to force the antidote in her mouth. Gabriell was glad to get it. The antidote should take over the poison in Gabriell's body in a few minutes. She would be back to her healthy self before she knew it.

"While we are waiting for my antidote to work, I am going to take both of you to my lab," Slash told Gabriell and Courtney while looking at them. "Gabriell can make more energy for me there. If everything goes as I planned, then I will give Courtney the antidote. That is as long as Gabriell makes the energy for me and it works perfectly. Understand?"

"Yes," Gabriell and Courtney answered in a low voice.

Gabriell and Courtney didn't want to go anywhere with Slash, let alone help him conquer the world, but what choice did they have at the moment?

"Good," said Slash, confident that everything was going to work just as he had planned. "Now get up and follow me to my lab. Try anything and you will die. Got it?"

Gabriell and Courtney nodded their heads and got up from under the bed. Then Slash took them to his lab.

At the lab, Slash told Gabriell to sit at his desk and told Courtney to lie on the bed next to the window. Slash motioned with his gun, and the girls followed his orders.

Slash's lab was like a regular room because all his chemicals for experiments were in his closet behind the desk. The walls were painted brown. They were all bare, except for one poster on the left wall. The poster had a periodical table on it and some names of special compounds and chemicals that weren't included in the periodical table. The only luxury in the room besides the bed and desk was an armchair. It was against the right wall, which was next to a window. Gabriell and Courtney were still upstairs with Slash, so they couldn't use that window for escapement either if they ever got the chance. The rest of the room was empty, except for the dark-brown carpet on the floor.

Slash went up to Courtney and tied her to the bed. Then he went over to Gabriell and put his gun against her neck. It was a solid black revolver that looked brand-new, even though it was five years old.

Gabriell was getting very scared. She was terrified that Slash was going to accidently pull the trigger and kill her. Gabriell knew that she would have to follow Slash's biding from here on out. She hated the idea of helping him, but she didn't have a choice at the moment.

"The antidote has taken full effect now," said Slash to Gabriell, happy with himself. "You should be fine now, so let's get to work on that experiment of yours about making me stronger and more powerful."

Gabriell was back to her normal self again. The antidote had work, but now she was forced to obey Slash's orders. She knew he was going to use it to help him kill lots of people. This was not the way Gabriell had pictured her experiment being used. She had planned to use it for good, not evil. If only she could stop this from happening, but what could she do?

"Now give me the ingredients you need to make more energy for me," Slash ordered Gabriell while she tried to think of something that she could do that wouldn't make him suspicious of her. Then an idea popped into Gabriell's head, and it was the perfect idea she had ever thought of. She was confident that her idea would work. Her idea was to change some of the ingredients in her experiment so that Slash would only be strong for a minute and then he would get weak. Then Gabriell and Courtney could escape from his clutches and hopefully get away from his evil house safe and sound. Gabriell hoped and prayed that her plan would work. It was the only chance Gabriell and Courtney had.

CHAPTER XV

Mike and his friends were on the road. They were heading to Slash's house. Mike was driving. Glenn was still sitting beside him. He was looking at his map, making sure that they were on Dark Street. Ayla and Erica were still in the back. They were looking out the window at the scenery outside. There wasn't much to see but houses and lots of trees. The sky was starting to get cloudy. It looked like it was going to rain soon. Ayla and Erica hoped that it wouldn't rain because they didn't need anything to slow them down from finding Gabriell and Courtney. Ayla and her friends hoped and prayed that their friends were okay.

"We are almost there!" said Mike, trying to get his friends' attention.

"I hope we are not too late," said Ayla, worried about Courtney and Gabriell.

"Me too," said Erica, also worried.

"We all hope that," said Glenn to Erica and Ayla, letting them know that they were worried about Gabriell and Courtney too. "Unfortunately, all we can do is hope for the best right now, and if something has happened, we will just have to deal with it and pray that everything will be okay."

"I guess you are right," Erica admitted to Glenn.

"I see the house!" said Mike, excited, while interrupting Ayla, Glenn, and Erica's conversation. "There is big problem though."

"What is it?" said Erica, concerned.

"Look at the house," said Mike, trying to explain the problem. "It is swarming with people that have guns in their hands."

"What are we going to do then?" said Ayla, looking at the house covered with guards.

"We can hide my car in the woods over there," said Mike, pointing to some trees on his right. "Then we can think of a plan that will get us in the house."

"Good idea," said Glenn, wondering how they were going to get into the house with all the guards surrounding it. "Let's get to it so we can hurry up and save our friends!"

"I totally agree," said Erica and Ayla with a smile. "Let's annihilate those guards!"

Mike parked his car in the woods behind Slash's house. Then they got out of his car. They hid behind some trees close to Slash's house and tried to figure out how they were going to get into the house.

"Any ideas?" said Mike to his friends while trying to concentrate on the matter at hand. "Something that we know will work."

Mike and his friends thought of some ideas for a few minutes. They hoped that the plan that they choose would be the right one, not the one that would backfire and get them in all kinds of trouble. No matter what the plan becomes, they know that it will be very dangerous and that their friends' lives depend on what they do from here on out.

"Huddle up," Ayla said to her friends, feeling confident. "I have an idea that just might work, but we must work as a team in order to do it. We also must use our special powers as an advantage to us so we can save Gabriell and Courtney. Now do you want to hear my idea?"

Ayla's friends nodded their heads in approval. They couldn't wait to hear her plan and save their friends from the rotten wooden house they saw before them.

"Yes," said Mike to Ayla, wondering what her plan was.

"Okay," said Ayla while looking at her friends with a smile on her face.

Ayla was truly happy with her plan. She knew it would work perfectly as long as everybody did what they were told. Ayla just hoped that they would be in time to save Gabriell and Courtney.

"First, I will use my mind to get the guns away from those men standing against the house. Glenn, you guard everybody. Make sure you get shot and not them."

"Oh, that's comforting," Glenn remarked while interrupting Ayla. "Now I got to risk my life out there!"

"Trust in your power! I know we can do this if we work as a team! Just listen to my plan, okay?" said Ayla, getting frustrated with Glenn because he wouldn't give her a chance to talk.

"Now, like I was saying before I was so rudely interrupted," said Ayla while narrowing her eyes toward Glenn. "Glenn, remember that the bullets will bounce off you! Don't be afraid of them!"

"Oh, that's easy for you to say!" Glenn remarked while interrupting Ayla once more.

"Please, Glenn, we have to do it this way, or we will not be able to save Gabriell and Courtney!" She wanted to hit Glenn because he was really getting on her nerves. "My plan won't work without you! We have to work together if we want to succeed!"

"Okay, fine, just get on with it!" said Glenn, finally agreeing with Ayla.

"Thank you," said Ayla, glad that she could finally finish telling her friends her scheme without getting rudely interrupted, or at least she hoped so. But who knows when Glenn was standing right beside her? Gabriell and Courtney will probably be dead by the time Ayla finishes telling everybody about her plan to save them if Glenn keeps up at the rate he is going. Hopefully, he was finished though.

"Now as I was saying," said Ayla, trying to remember what she needed to say next to her friends, "once we go into the house, Glenn will be the leader and protect us, which I hope I don't regret. Mike and Erica, you just need to use your powers whenever you think we need them. Got it?"

"Yes," said Mike while Erica and Glenn nodded their heads in approval.

"Good," said Ayla, glad that they could now put their plan to work. "Let's get to it!"

"Wwwait!" said Glenn, not quite ready to get started with Ayla's plan.

"What!" yelled Ayla, really wanting to hurt Glenn now.

"So you mean that I am going to have to stand in front of everybody like I am a statue or something and let them guards shoot at me all they want?" said Glenn, trying to get everything clear.

"That's exactly what you are going to do," said Ayla, narrowing her eyes straight toward Glenn.

"Well, okay, but if my power fails and I get shot at, you are dead," said Glenn, not so sure about his power.

"Don't worry," said Ayla, trying to make Glenn feel better about himself. "Your power is fine. Just do what you have to do in order to keep us safe and to help save our friends that are trapped in that dungeon over there."

"Okay," said Glenn, starting to feel a little better about his power. "I'll do my best."

"You do that," said Ayla, patting Glenn on the back. "Now let's get this plan in gear!"

Ayla and her friends walked through the woods and stood behind some bushes next to Slash's house. They looked around Slash's house and saw two guards with guns. The two guards were blocking the entrance to Slash's home. Both of the guards were dressed in camouflage. The one on the right side of the door of the house was a man. His arms were covered with tattoos. He was in his mid-forties with grayish red hair on his forehead. The man also had yellow eyes. He was very tall, about seven foot. He had a bad scar on his face, and Ayla and her friends had no clue how it got there. The man also had one hickey on his neck, where some woman had kissed him the night before. It was gross! And another thing that was gross was that he had an earring in his nose and his mouth. They couldn't see how in the world he could talk, let alone kiss a woman!

The guard beside the man was a woman in her twenties. Ayla and her friends hoped that she wasn't the woman that kissed the man because if she was, then she needed some serious help since he was totally sick. That was according to Ayla and her friends anyway.

The woman had short brown hair and beautiful hazel eyes. She was also tall and very appealing to a man because of her looks. The woman had one gold earring in each ear that was fake, but they looked real. She even had a tattoo on her arm that would catch a guy's attention because it had "I love you" on it. Aside from her looks, she looked mean and serious. The same went for the man sitting beside her. They both had guns held firm in their hands. They were ready to shoot anybody that came close to Slash's house. By the look on their faces, Ayla and her friends could tell that they were not afraid to shoot somebody.

"Okay," said Ayla to her friends while looking at the two guards standing at the door to Slash's home. "Once I have got the guns away from the guards, Erica and Mike, you will then knock out the guards while they are stunned. Then we can sneak into the house and go from there," Ayla said, explaining her plan of action to her friends.

Erica, Mike, and Glenn told Ayla that they were ready. Then Ayla focused her mind on the guns in the two guards' hands while Erica and Mike gradually moved toward the guards. The guards had no idea of what was about to happen. The guns moved a little in their hands, but they ignored them. They thought it was just their imagination. Unfortunately for them, it was not their imagination. Their guns were really moving on their own with the help of Ayla's mind. Ayla proved that the guns were moving by making them move once more, but this time, they slipped right through the two guards' hands. Then the guns sailed through the air as if they were being carried by the wind, but there was no wind to carry them.

"Hey, what's going on here?" said the female guard, surprised and bewildered.

"They're ... they're coming to ... to life!" stuttered the male guard.

"No kidding," said the female guard, scared.

While the guards were watching, stunned, the guns floated straight through the bushes and landed right into Ayla's hands.

"Cool!" said Glenn, starting to really like Ayla's power. "That was using your head. You are going to have to show me that trick of yours one day."

"Maybe I will, but now we must focus on saving Gabriell and Courtney. Take this," said Ayla, handing Glenn a gun while watching Mike and Erica. They were about to pounce on their enemies.

"Okay," said Glenn while examining the gun that he now held in his hand. It was a .22-caliber rifle with six brand-new bullets in it. It was a nice gun, but Glenn wasn't sure that he could use it. He was afraid to kill somebody, even someone that truly deserved to be killed. Ayla, on the other hand, was okay with a gun. She was not afraid to use it. Her philosophy was, if you have to use it, then use it. That plain and simple.

While Ayla and Glenn were hiding in the bushes, Erica and Mike went to work on their job, beating up the enemies. They slowly edged closer and closer to the two guards. The guards had no clue that two people were behind them, ready to attack. Erica took care of the man, while Mike had the woman. Erica tapped the man to get his attention. Then the man looked at her and stared. She ignored his look and went straight for his leg with a left side kick that made the man fall flat on the ground. Then she punched the guy with a left hook that landed right on the man's face. That finished the guy off.

"The bigger they are, the harder they fall," said Erica, quite pleased with herself, while looking at the guy lying on the floor beside her. "You are not so tough now, are you?" The man just lay there, bewildered. He was still stunned by her moves and his gun moving on its own.

Mike made the woman dizzy and faint by running ten circles around her really fast. Then the woman fell to the ground with a thud. Mike was quite pleased with himself too. He looked at the woman lying on the ground and saw that she wasn't so tough and scary anymore. She and the man were now both scaredy-cats.

"Way to go!" yelled Glenn to Erica and Mike while walking out from behind the bushes with Ayla.

"You showed them," said Ayla, proud of Mike and Erica.

"Thanks," said Mike and Erica with a smile on both their faces. They were both very proud of themselves.

Mike and his friends gave each other high fives. They were proud of their first win against the enemies, but their adventure wasn't over yet. They still had many dangers and enemies to face as they ventured into the house. Were they prepared and ready for the dangers that awaited them up ahead? Were their powers up to the challenge, or would their powers fail them when they needed them the most?

CHAPTER XVI

Gabriell was working hard on the experiment for Slash so he could become almighty and powerful. What Slash didn't know yet was that he would become weaker instead, thanks to Gabriell being a scientist and knowing how to make a foolproof potion. She knew exactly which ingredients had to be changed in order for her foolproof potion to work, but could she pull it off?

Gabriell had all the ingredients that she needed. They were on the desk beside her. The ingredients were from nitrogen to feathers from rare birds. Gabriell began to add and mix some of the ingredients into a flask and a test tube. She poured the ingredients in a test tube first to measure it. Then once she had the right amount of each ingredient, she poured it into the flask beside her and stirred it together with a metal stick.

Slash watched Gabriell very carefully, trying to learn how to make the potion so he could make more of it on his own when he needed to. Unfortunately for Slash, he had no idea that he was wasting his time watching Gabriell make her experiment since she was making a foolproof potion just for him.

Courtney was still on the bed, latched up. She was beginning to really suffer from the poison that was forced into her mouth. She was hurting all over. She hoped that she could fight off the toxin until help came. She prayed that somebody would come and save her before it was too late for both of them to be rescued. Would Ayla and her friends get to Gabriell and Courtney in time to save them, especially Courtney?

Meanwhile, Ayla and her friends were in Slash's house, looking around. The first room they saw was the den. It was a pretty large room. There was a couch in the right corner of the room and a television in the other corner of the room. The couch and television were covered with dust. Nobody had dusted them in months, maybe even years. The couch was black and worn-out with holes in it. There was a table in front of the couch. There were two glasses on the table that were half-filled with red wine. In the middle of the table was a dish with a biscuit on it. A piece of the biscuit had been bitten. With the food and drinks on the table, it looked like two people had just left the room a few minutes ago in a hurry. The carpet on the floor of the den was off-white. It was filled with dirt and mud from outside. The walls in the den were painted brown. They were bare, except for two pictures hanging in the middle of the wall that were to the right of the television set. One of the pictures was of an eerie full moon with dark woods below. The other picture showed an old pirate man. He had a pirate hat on him and a white sailor shirt. The man had a gray beard and gray hair to match. He even had one eye, like Blackbeard, the pirate.

After Ayla and her friends had finished examining the den, they walked into the weapon room. It was a small room that had lots of cabinets in it. There were guns and bullets in them. Ayla and her friends got a couple of guns out of the cabinets and put some extra bullets in them. Now they all had a gun to protect themselves with. There wasn't nothing else in the room that they could use, so they headed into the hallway, walking very quietly and cautiously though the rooms, trying to not make a sound because they didn't want nobody to see them. Ayla and her friends didn't want to fight any more people than they had to.

Glenn was leading the pack, protecting them just in case they get shot at by somebody. Glenn and his friends were all holding guns firm in their hands, but they promised each other that they wouldn't use them unless they had to. They didn't want to kill their enemy when they could throw him or her in jail and make them suffer even more for their crime. Furthermore, if they did use the guns, all the guards in the house would come running toward them, and they would be surrounded by guards. Then they would more than likely be forced to surrender, and they would get themselves trapped in the house forever with Gabriell and Courtney, so they must only use their guns as a last resort.

Once Glenn and his friends had walked through a long hallway of bare walls, they were stopped by ten men with guns in their hands. They were preventing Glenn and his friends from going upstairs where Gabriell and Courtney were. Glenn and his friends were surrounded. Seeing the situation in hand, Ayla used her powers to get the guns quickly out of the guards' hands.

"What the hell!" said one of the men, shocked as his gun flew out of his hand.

Ayla and her friends threw their guns down and started to fight the guards. They didn't want to make too much noise because they couldn't deal with anymore guards than they were facing already. Glenn and his friends were already outnumbered, and that meant that they had less of a chance of winning this battle. Would they be able to kick these guys' butts and continue on up the stairs to rescue their friends?

CHAPTER XVII

"Follow my lead!" Mike yelled to his friends while trying to get their attention. An idea had just popped into his head that might just save them from these guards whom they were being forced to fight at that very moment. Then Mike looked up at the ceiling of Slash's house and said, "Look, the ceiling is cracking!"

The stupid guards were fooled by Mike's trick. All of them looked straight up at the ceiling of Slash's house, trying to find whatever Mike saw, but Mike didn't see anything. He was just trying to get their attention so they could have an advantage over them. Now Mike and his friends could sneak up on the guards and beat them up. His diversion had worked perfectly.

They started attacking the guards while they had the chance. Erica got to work beating up guys with her karate moves. She was good at it too. One guy came up to her and tried to make her fall by doing a sweep kick on her. Erica jumped right over his leg and kicked him hard in the stomach.

"Ouch!" the guy exclaimed as he fell to the ground.

"I show you a thing or two, didn't I?" said Erica to the guard while looking down on him with a smile. The man nodded his head and fainted. "Well, that takes care of one man. Only nine to go!"

"Only!" yelled Ayla as she was being trapped by two men in a corner. "Oh, that's reassuring."

"Sorry, just trying to be confident," said Erica as she headed toward Ayla, seeing that she needed help.

Ayla didn't need any help from Erica though. She had her situation under control when she saw the object she needed to knock the guys out who were trying to trap her. It was a piece of pottery on a glass table that was almost behind the two guards who were cornering her. She ignored the guards and concentrated on the piece of pottery. It started to move around on the table. Then the piece of pottery slowly rose off the table and floated toward the two guards who were surrounding her. The piece of pottery slowly moved toward its victims.

"Hey, what are you doing?" one of the guards said to Ayla, noticing that she was concentrating on something.

Ayla ignored the guard and made the piece of pottery hit the back of both of the guards' heads with her mind. The men fell to the ground with a thud. They were both knocked out cold by the piece of pottery.

"That one was for Gabriell!" Ayla exclaimed to the unconscious men lying on the ground beside her.

"I see that you didn't need my help after all," said Erica to Ayla, glad that she had no problem getting rid of the two guards.

"Nope," said Ayla, glad that her power worked so well for her in the situation that she was just in. "I made very good use of my power, and so did you."

"You got that right!" exclaimed Erica while really starting to enjoy this feeling. "We can really tear these guys up with our powers. I am so glad we have them. I don't know what we would do without them."

"Nothing, but get kidnapped ourselves," said Ayla to Erica, admitting the truth.

"Yeah, no kidding," said Erica with a little laugh.

While Erica and Ayla were getting ready to beat up some more guards, Mike made a man dizzy by running circles around him just like the female guard he knocked out outside of Slash's house. The only difference was that Mike ran faster around the man than he did the female guard. Making sure the man would faint from getting so dizzy.

"Well, that takes care of him," said Mike, happy of his victory.

Mike, Ayla, and Erica did not have much trouble knocking out the men that attacked them. Glenn, on the other hand, was having a serious dilemma. He was outnumbered by three to one. Three guards were trying to corner him just like two guards had done to Ayla. He couldn't really use his secret power because his body was just a shield. Objects would bounce off it. That power couldn't help him much right now. At least that was the way it seemed to be at the moment, but then Glenn thought of a great idea. He could convince the guards to throw something at him. The objects would bounce off his body, and he wouldn't get hurt. This would make the guards mad so Glenn could defeat them, but could he trick all the guards who were surrounding him at that very moment? He would try his best to.

"I dare you to throw something at me," Glenn said, trying to get the three guards' attention. "Come on, don't tell me you're chicken! Cock! Cock!" said Glenn, trying to imitate a chicken. He was doing a very good job of it, and he was definitely convincing the three guards to throw something at him.

"Okay, you've asked for it," said one of the guards as he and his fellow comrades picked up some heavy bricks from the fireplace and threw them at Glenn. They threw the bricks with all their might.

Glenn was scared. He knew that he couldn't dodge all three of the bricks. He didn't know if his power could stand up to the test. He now regretted that he ever called the men chicken as he saw the bricks coming at him.

Would his power save him from getting hurt, or would his power fail him? That was the big question now. It ran though Glenn's head as the bricks came closer and closer to him. He tried to dodge the bricks, but unfortunately, one hit him on the foot. Before he knew what had happened, the brick bounced off his foot and went straight toward one of the guards who hit him. As Glenn began to realize what had just happened, a big smile came over his face. He was relieved that his power didn't fail him, and better yet, the brick was going toward one of the guards, but it wasn't over yet.

"Huh?" said one of the guards, puzzled by the brick that was coming straight toward him. The man was stunned, he couldn't move. The brick hit him right on the stomach. The man fell straight to the ground once the brick hit him. He was knocked out cold. The other two guards looked at their comrade on the floor and then looked at Glenn with a mean and serious look on their faces.

"You are dead, kid!" exclaimed one of the guards.

The guard was steamed, and Glenn could tell it. The smile went immediately off Glenn's face. He was really scared now, and he seriously doubted that somebody punching him or kicking him would not hurt him. Glenn knew he was in serious trouble now, but then he remembered his friends who were fighting the guards too. He hollered for their help and prayed that they would come to his rescue.

Would Glenn's friends be able to help him, or would they be tied up fighting other guards? What would Glenn do if his friends couldn't come help him? Those questions pondered through Glenn's head as he saw the two guards coming toward him.

CHAPTER XVIII

Erica was beating up a guy by punching and kicking him with her karate moves. She was making very good use of her ability. Her power gave her a great advantage over the men she fought. She hoped and prayed that she would always have this ability so she could protect herself from people who want to hurt her, like the guards who were fighting her at that very moment.

While Erica was knocking out the guy, she thought she heard somebody call for help. She finished the guy off with a high kick that landed right in the man's face. Then she stood still and listened, trying to find out if somebody really was in trouble. Maybe it was Gabriell or Courtney.

"Help!" Glenn exclaimed as the men came closer to him.

"Nobody can help you now, kid," exclaimed one of the guards, grinning from ear to ear.

Erica heard Glenn call for help. She ran toward his voice, hoping that he was not in too much danger. Unfortunately, Glenn was in terrible danger. The two guards were cornering him against the wall. They were ready to beat him up, and there was nothing Glenn could do. He was trapped with no place to go for safety.

One of the guards grabbed Glenn and held him tight. The guard made sure he wouldn't get away from his grasp. Then the other guard went behind Glenn and put his arm around his neck. He was attempting to choke him until he fainted or died. And just as Glenn had feared, the man's arm did not bounce off his neck. He was in real trouble now. All he could do was call for help and try his best to hold on as long as he could for the sake of his family and friends. He hoped that someone would save him before it was too late.

Erica ran as fast as she could. She found Glenn being choked by one guard and another guard holding him down. She saw that Glenn was struggling and doing the best he could to stay alive.

Glenn fought and tried to get free from both guards' clutches, but they were too strong. Glenn could not get away from them no matter how hard he tried. He was losing the fight fast. Erica was his only hope.

Erica knew she had to hurry and save Glenn. She snuck up behind the man who was choking him. Erica made sure that the man's mind was concentrated on Glenn and not on his back. She walked as slowly and quietly as she could toward the man. She was trying to be as quiet as a mouse and as slick as a cat.

Erica edged closer to the man and slowly reached for the his neck. She was very careful not to make a sound. Then as Erica got her arms close to the man's neck, she quickly grabbed it and used her arms to choke him. Erica was taking a risk not knowing if her ability would give her strength to break the guy's grip. Erica winced as the guy slowly loosened his grip on Glenn. She just hoped that Glenn would be okay.

The man tried to fall toward Glenn and the person who was holding him. Erica stopped the man and laid him on the ground. He was knocked out cold but not dead.

While Erica was laying the man on the ground, the man's comrade came toward her. She had no idea that somebody was behind her and ready and willing to kill her. Thank goodness Mike saw what was about to happen to her, but he couldn't help her since he was tied up with fighting someone himself. Instead, Mike called out her name and told her that somebody was about to attack her.

Erica heard Mike's warning and quickly moved away from harm by doing a cartwheel over the man who was knocked out cold on the floor. She got away from the guy just in the nick of time. Then the guard ran toward her.

Once the man got to Erica, she hit him as hard as she could with a right punch. The punched landed on the man's face. The punch made the guard dizzy, but he still was standing. Erica punched him one final time, and the guy fell to the ground with a bang. Then she told Mike thanks for the warning and checked on Glenn to see if he was okay.

"Are you okay?" Erica asked Glenn, worried.

Glenn was on the floor, resting. He had almost choked to death, but thanks to Erica, he was okay.

"Yes," said Glenn, glad to be alive. "I am fine. I just need to catch my breath. Thank you for saving my life. I thought I was a goner. I'm not sure if I want to be a hero anymore. I don't like the idea of risking my life to save somebody else's."

"We knew this would be dangerous, but we are doing this for our friends," Erica said, trying to convince Glenn that they could not give up for Gabriell's and Courtney's sake. "We are the only ones that can save them. They are counting on us. We must not stop now. We are too close to winning the battle."

"Yes, we are very close to victory," said Ayla, joining Erica and Glenn's conversation. "I have this feeling that the answer to all our questions is upstairs. It's the only explanation for all those guys attacking us."

"I guess you are both right," said Glenn, feeling better about the situation they were in with trying to save Gabriell and Courtney. "I just hope that we are not too late."

"Yes, I hope for that too," said Ayla, really worried about their friends. She knew they had to be in great danger if they were alive.

"I believe that's all of them for now," Mike said while joining his friends who were looking at the stairs that they must go up now in order to save their friends. Their hardest task awaited them up above.

"Let's head on up the stairs and hope that Gabriell and Courtney are waiting for us to save them once we reach the top," said Erica while looking up the flight of stairs. She wondered what dangers were lurking up above and waiting for them.

Erica, Mike, Ayla, and Glenn went upstairs. They hoped that Gabriell and Courtney were up there and not somewhere else in the house that they hadn't looked yet. Were Gabriell and Courtney okay, or were they too late? Were they ready for the major dangers that lied ahead of them? Were their powers powerful enough to withstand what's to come of them?

CHAPTER XIX

Gabriell was still working hard on the experiment, but she would be done in a few minutes. Courtney was getting weaker and weaker as time passed by. How much longer would she be able to hold on? The potion had been in her body for six hours now. She only had five hours to live without a cure. Would she last long enough for somebody to make an antidote for her if somebody was lucky enough to make it?

Gabriell was stirring up the last bit of ingredients that she needed for the potion in a flask. She could not believe that the experiment for Slash was almost done. It seemed like just a few minutes ago, Slash had started gathering chemicals Gabriell needed to make more energy for him. Now she was about to give the formula to someone that might be the evilest person alive! All she could do now was pray that her foolproof potion would work to her and Courtney's advantage.

"My work is done," Gabriell told Slash, hoping everything would go as she had planned.

Slash grabbed the experiment out of Gabriell's hand, looked at it for a second, and then swallowed all of it. Courtney and Gabriell saw the substance go down his throat. Courtney was scared. She was afraid that Slash might hurt them now that he would be powerful and almighty. Courtney feared that Slash might even kill them now that he had what he needed to dominate the world! There was no reason left to keep them alive.

In a few minutes, Gabriell would find out if her potion worked. She hoped that he would get so weak that she and Courtney could slip right by him and escape out of the room. Would her plan work, or would her experiment backfire on her?

Meanwhile, Glenn and his friends were upstairs. They searched through some rooms, trying to find Gabriell and Courtney, but they didn't have any luck at the moment. They hoped to find their friends soon.

Glenn and his friends decided to hide behind a curtain where nobody could see them. Glenn saw one last door that they hadn't searched yet. Two guards were guarding the door. They were blocking the entrance to where Gabriell and Courtney was. They were the same two people that carried their friends into the room. The two guards looked as mean and serious as ever.

"That must be the door where Gabriell and Courtney are," said Glenn, looking at the guards. "It is the only door that we haven't searched."

"You're right," said Ayla to Glenn, happy that they were finally about to get out of this place, hopefully with everybody safe and sound. "Let's slaughter those guys and go save Gabriell and Courtney!"

Ayla's friends agreed with her. They ran toward the two guards and began to beat them up. Before they knew it, the two guys were knocked out.

"That was too easy," said Mike, getting worried.

"Yeah, no kidding," said Erica. "Do you think we could be going right into a trap?"

"I hope not, but we can't just sit here and wait," said Ayla, wanting to knock down the door so she could save her friends. "We must find out if Gabriell and Courtney are okay, and if they are not, we must rescue them before it is too late!"

"But what if we are already too late and it is a trap?" asked Mike, concerned for himself and his friends.

"We just have to take that risk," said Ayla, wanting desperately for Gabriell and Courtney to be okay.

"I guess you are right," said Mike. "Let's get this door open so we can see what's behind it."

Mike went up to the door and tried to open it, but the door was locked as tight as a drum.

"The door won't budge," said Mike, trying to get the door open with all his might.

"May I?" Erica insisted, wanting to show off her power.

"Go ahead," said Mike. He didn't think Erica could knock down the door. "Take your best shot at it."

"I will," said Erica, glaring at Mike with confidence.

"Hiiijah!" said Erica as she kicked the door down with a powerful, high left kick.

"Ayla, Erica, Glenn, Mike, you're here!" shouted Gabriell. She was so happy to see her friends.

Slash turned his head to see who Gabriell was talking to. He was not surprised to see some people finally come and try to save Gabriell and Courtney. Slash was glad that he now had some people to fight so he could test out Gabriell's experiment. He was so confident that he could stop Gabriell and Courtney's friends from saving them in a flat second since he had drunk the potion that Gabriell was forced to make for him. Too bad he didn't know that Gabriell had given him her foolproof potion. Plus, he didn't even have the slightest clue that Ayla and her friends had secret powers, neither did Gabriell or Courtney.

"So, you've come to save your friends," said Slash, glaring at Ayla and her friends.

"Yes, we have," said Ayla, ready to save Gabriell and Courtney from the evil guy facing her and her friends at that very moment.

"Well, go ahead and try to take me, but if you do not beat me, you and all your friends will perish with Gabriell and her friend," said Slash, feeling more confident than he ever had in his whole life. "I must warn you though. Gabriell has given me her little experiment. You do not have a chance against me, thanks to your dear friend over there, but if you want to save your friends even though they have betrayed you, go ahead and take your best shot at me."

"I didn't betray anyone. I was forced to make the potion," said Gabriell to her friends, trying to get them to believe her.

"We know you didn't," said Ayla, trying to see if Gabriell was really okay, but Slash was blocking her. "I will toast this guy just for forcing you to make your experiment for him."

Ayla focused on Slash's desk that was almost behind him. The legs began to vibrate as they were slowly lifted off the ground by Ayla's mind. Then the wooden desk soared up into the air and went straight toward Slash.

Gabriell and Courtney had stoned faces. They could not believe that they were seeing a desk move on its own, but then they realized how hard Ayla had her eyes focused on the object. They started to wonder if Ayla was making the desk move somehow, but how could she move the desk without touching it? That's what puzzled Gabriell and Courtney.

"Does Ayla have telekinesis?" Courtney asked Gabriell as she came over to unlatch her from the bed. "Is that possible?"

"I don't know, but I would love to be able to move things without touching them," said Gabriell, fascinated by Ayla's secret power.

"Me too!"

Courtney was relieved to finally get the restraints off her body, but the poison was still in her. She was really getting sick from the poison that was invading her body. The substance had been in her body for seven hours now. Would somebody be able to make an antidote for her before she died from the toxin?

In the meantime, Ayla and her friends were trying to beat up Slash, so they could get Gabriell and Courtney to safety. They did not know about Courtney's condition. Would they be able to save their friends and get Courtney an antidote?

Slash saw the desk coming straight toward him and said, "I don't know how you are moving things, but it doesn't matter. You can't stop me. I am invincible!" He was still very confident that nothing could hurt him.

The desk came closer and closer toward Slash's body. It was heading directly toward his stomach and neck. Slash just stood still at the spot on the floor as if his shoes were glued to it. He was not scared at all. Slash was convinced that the desk would not hurt him since he had Gabriell's potion in him. And sure enough, the object did not harm him. It just bounced right off his body and didn't even leave a mark on him!

When the desk bounced off Slash's body, it went straight toward Ayla. Luckily, she saw the object coming. She was able to dodge it just in the nick of time.

"That was too close," said Ayla as she saw the desk fly by her and hit the wall. "How did that happen? The piece of furniture should have stopped him cold. Besides, Gabriell didn't tell anybody that her experiment could do this."

"I don't know," said Glenn, puzzled. "The desk just bounced off him as if he had my secret power."

"Then his power must be just like Glenn's," said Erica, getting an idea in her head. "I can defeat him with my karate moves in no time."

"Go ahead," said Mike, agreeing with Erica. "It's worth a try."

Erica nodded her head and glanced at Mike. Then she went up to Slash. Erica hoped that she could defeat him with her own special power. To start off, Erica decided to try a right kick and land it hard on Slash's face. She was hoping to knock him out with one blow. The kick she used was the roundhouse, the kick she had learned so quickly and easily in her karate class, thanks to her special power.

Erica gathered all her strength and hit Slash as hard as she could with the roundhouse kick. She aimed for his head, one of the most vulnerable parts of the human body. Amazingly though, when the kick hit Slash in the face, it didn't even stun him. He was not fazed one bit. Slash just shook his head, stood there at his spot, and began to laugh his dark, evil laugh.

"Ha ha ha," said Slash about his easy victory against Erica and her friends. "You can't even get a dent on me. You have truly lost this battle. Now you and your friends will perish with Gabriell and Courtney."

Gabriell and Courtney saw that their friends had lost the battle. Her foolproof experiment had failed her, but she couldn't understand what could have gone wrong. Gabriell had done everything she could to the potion to make sure it would work to her advantage and not Slash's. She sat there on the bed and watched everything begin to fall into pieces. She wanted to cry, but she knew that she must not for her friends' sake.

Slash was happy that he had won the battle, but then something strange began to happen. All of sudden, something came over him. He stopped laughing and made a confused face at Ayla and her friends.

"Gabriell," said Courtney with a little smile, trying to get Gabriell's attention, "look at Slash. I think something is wrong with him."

Gabriell picked up her head and looked at Slash. Then as she looked at him, she began to realize that her foolproof experiment had finally started to work. She put on a big smile and said, "I did it!"

"What worked?" said Courtney to Gabriell, puzzled.

"I made my experiment foolproof," said Gabriell, trying to explain what she had done.

"Way to go, Gabriell," said Courtney, happy for her friend's victory.

Meanwhile, Ayla and her friends had no idea of what was happening to Slash. They began to watch him make faces. They were totally bewildered by what was happening.

"What is wrong with him?" said Glenn, confused.

"I don't know," said Mike, also surprised by Slash's reactions.

"Hey!" said Erica, getting an idea in her head. "Now we have the chance to defeat Slash while he has his attention on himself. Let's beat this guy up and help our friends escape from this horrible place."

"Yeah, you are right, Erica," said Mike, putting a big smile on his face. "Let's do it!"

"Yes!" said Ayla and Glenn, smiling at each other.

Ayla, Erica, Mike, and Glenn surrounded Slash from all sides. They made sure there was no way for Slash to get away from them. He was in the center, trapped. Glenn and his friends began to work as a team. They used all their secret powers to defeat Slash.

"I am getting weaker," said Slash, not understanding what was happening to him as Erica hit him with a low kick. "What's going on here?"

"Yes!" shouted Gabriell, excited about her foolproof plan. It was really taking a toll on Slash, and Gabriell loved it. "My scheme is working just the way I had planned!"

"What are you talking about?" said Ayla to Gabriell, turning her head away from the fight at hand.

"I tell you later. Just defeat Slash so we can get out of here," said Gabriell, anxious to get out of Slash's home and get an antidote for Courtney.

"Okay," said Ayla, wondering exactly what Gabriell had done to Slash.

Ayla and her friends continued to beat up Slash using all their special powers. Gabriell and Courtney watched them fight. They were amazed and puzzled by their friends, wondering how they became so powerful. Gabriell and Courtney saw that each of them had different special powers. They were fascinated by all their powers, especially by Ayla's. They thought it was so cool that she could move objects without touching them. Gabriell and Courtney also began to get curious about where their friends' powers came from and how they got those special powers.

Mike ran around Slash very fast and made him dizzy, while Erica punched and kicked him hard with her body. Glenn and Ayla also helped their friends. They stopped guards from coming in to help Slash defeat them. Glenn shielded his friends by letting himself get shot at since the bullets bounced right off him. Ayla focused on objects to knock out the guards with who tried to come into the room.

It didn't take too long for Erica and Mike to defeat Slash, thanks to Gabriell's foolproof plan. Erica finished Slash off with a high punch right on Slash's neck. Mike made sure Slash went down and stayed down by doing a knee kick he had learned in karate class. By Erica and Mike combining their two special powers, they defeated Slash.

"You did it!" said Ayla and Glenn with smiles on their faces. They had just finished defeating the guards.

"No, we did it!" said Erica to her friends, smiling. "We worked as a team and won. Now we can finally save our friends and get out of this awful place."

Erica, Mike, Glenn, and Ayla gave each other high fives and went toward Gabriell and Courtney. They were pleased with their victory, but when Glenn and his friends got to Gabriell and Courtney, all they saw were sad faces.

"Why are you both so glum?" said Erica, concerned and bewildered by her friends. "We saved your lives. Aren't you going to say thank you?"

"I'm sorry," said Gabriell to her friends, looking at them sadly. "It is just that Courtney is really sick, and we have to get her an antidote soon."

"Why is she so sick?" asked Ayla.

"Slash forced a poison down her throat and mine that would make us weaker and weaker until we would die," said Gabriell, trying to explain what had happened to her and Courtney. "Slash gave me the antidote as soon as Courtney promised him that I would make my experiment for him. Then I made my formula foolproof as you've noticed to get him back for hurting Courtney and me. I can make the antidote for Courtney, but I need time. Unfortunately, time is not on our side. She only has about four hours to live without the antidote. I am not sure if that is enough time for us to get out of here and for me to make the cure for her."

"Don't worry," said Ayla, trying to comfort Gabriell. "We will make sure you have enough time to make the antidote and save Courtney's life."

"I'll be fine, Gabriell," said Courtney, trying to cheer up her friend. "There will be plenty of time for you to make the cure for me."

Courtney told Gabriell those things for her benefit. She was feeling bad, but she didn't want to worry Gabriell. Courtney wasn't sure that Gabriell would be able to make the antidote for her in time, even though Gabriell was a scientist. She was scared for her own self, but she tried not to show it because she didn't want to put any more pressure on her friend. Courtney knew that Gabriell might mess up the antidote if she was rushed into making it.

Ayla went up to Courtney. Courtney was still lying on the bed that Slash had restrained her to. She had a very sad complexion on her face. Her face was pale, and her cheeks were red. Ayla could tell that Courtney was very sick. She felt sorry for Courtney and wished that she and her friends came sooner so this would not had happened to her.

"How are you feeling?" Ayla asked Courtney, concerned.

"Weak, but I am okay for now," replied Courtney, glad that she and Gabriell were finally safe from Slash.

"Can you walk?" Ayla asked Courtney, wondering if she was strong enough.

"I can for a while, I think," said Courtney, not sure how long her strength would hold up, thanks to the poison Slash had gave her.

"Good," said Ayla to Courtney, relieved that she was okay right now. "Now let's get out of this evil house while the coast is clear."

All of Ayla's friends totally agreed with her, especially Gabriell and Courtney. They truly had enough of Slash's house, and they hoped and prayed that they would never see it again.

As Ayla and all her friends left the room, they prayed that they would get out of Slash's house safely without having to battle too many guards. They knew that the fight wasn't over yet. Ayla and all her friends still had many evil people to face. They prayed that they would not be stuck in the house forever because of all the guards.

"How did you all get those special powers that Courtney and I saw you use when you all were battling Slash?" Gabriell asked Ayla and her friends while traveling through Slash's house. Gabriell was wondering what the scoop was on their friends' special powers.

"Yes, how did you get them?" Courtney added, also wanting to know about their secret powers.

"You have to promise to keep our special abilities a secret if you want to hear a brief story about our special powers," said Mike to Gabriell and Courtney, trying to get them to understand.

"We promise," said Gabriell and Courtney to Mike.

"Good," said Mike, happy that he could trust Gabriell and Courtney. "The basic thing behind our story is that we got our powers from four aliens that looked like giant bugs. They came to earth in a spaceship that we found in the woods while we were traveling home from a group date that we had together. They talked to us in a foreign language that we had never heard before, and then each bug went up to one of us and bit us once. Then they flew away into the sky. That is how we think we got our special powers. I know the brief story I just told you sounded crazy, but it is the truth."

"We believe you, but how did you find the spaceship and the bugs?" Gabriell asked Mike, curious.

"Erica saw something fall from the sky while she was looking through my car window," said Mike, explaining what had happened to them in the past. "It appeared to be a meteorite, but she wanted to check it out to make sure, so we all got out of my car and went into the woods to see what had fallen from the sky. That's where we found a spaceship in place of what Erica had thought was a meteorite."

"Weren't you scared?" said Courtney, wondering while trying to ignore her body that was getting weaker.

"Yes, but we were too curious," said Mike, thinking about what had happened to him and his friends on that strange and wondrous night. "We had to find out for ourselves what was in the spaceship. We had never seen anything like it, so we had to check it out."

"Yeah, it was like someone was talking to us, wanting us to come inside," said Glenn, remembering the eerie night.

"I understand," said Courtney, fascinated by Mike's story. "Thanks for saving our lives back there."

"No problem!" said Glenn with a smile. "And don't worry, we will make sure you get the antidote you need."

"Thanks. I just hope I will be okay," said Courtney, worried. She had never felt so bad in her life.

"I'll make sure of it," said Gabriell, patting her worried friend on the back.

"Thanks," said Courtney, looking up at her friend with a slight smile on her face.

"Now that we have got that settled, let's find a way out of here before too many guards come after us," said Erica, ready to get out of Slash's house.

Mike and all of his friends stopped talking to each other and began to travel through more rooms. They headed toward the exit of Slash's house that was probably guarded well by his people.

As Mike and his friends were walking, some guards popped their heads out from some hidden corners in Slash's house. They jumped out and attacked Mike and his friends. The guards surrounded them from corner to corner. They were blocking the exit. They were making sure that no one would get out of Slash's house alive. All the guards wanted to kill Mike and his friends since they had killed their leader. It only was fitting.

Mike and his friends were hurdled in a circle. They were surrounded by enemies from all sides, twelve guards in all. They were outnumbered by six, and one of their people happened to be very vulnerable, which was Courtney, since she was so weak from the poison. Glenn decided to protect her from the guards by using his body as a shield. He made sure no harm was done to Courtney during the battle.

Mike, Ayla, and Erica used all their special powers to defeat the guards who attacked them, while Gabriell and Glenn grabbed everything they could to stop the evil people from hurting them. They used anything, from antique pottery to mirrors. Glenn and Gabriell made sure that Courtney was protected while they defended themselves from the guards.

At first, Ayla and her friends had no problem battling the men until the guards discovered their fatal flaw, Courtney. The guards that had not been defeated yet went straight toward Courtney. When Ayla, Mike, and Erica realized what was happening, they ran over to Glenn and Gabriell and helped them fight off the guards who were left to be defeated.

Courtney stayed close to her friends. She wished that she could help them, but knew that she probably didn't have enough strength to fight and last long enough for Gabriell to get the antidote in her.

Gabriell got in a tough situation while she was trying to protect her friend from getting hurt. Three of the guards had realized that Gabriell didn't have special powers, so they aimed straight for her. Gabriell fought them in any way she could by hitting them and throwing whatever she could find at them. She did not have a chance against the three men even though she fought with all her might. The guards were stronger and faster than Gabriell. They outnumbered her, three to one, and she knew it. The odds were against her, but Gabriell knew that she must try to defeat them for Courtney's sake.

The three guards made a circle around Gabriell. They blocked anyone from getting through them. Gabriell was trapped, and there was nothing she could do about it. Gabriell was scared, and she wasn't sure of what she could do to save herself from those evil men surrounding her.

The three guards stopped Gabriell from throwing any objects at them by blocking her from reaching all the objects she could throw at them so she had nothing to defend herself with. The guards realized that Gabriell couldn't do nothing to them, so they went up to her and started to beat her up. She tried to get away from them, but there was no hope for her. She even tried to use her arms as a shield to protect her body, but it didn't do her much good. Now Gabriell wished that she had taken karate or some kind of class that would have taught her how to defend herself from getting hurt so she would have a chance against the guys. Unfortunately, she had never taken karate before, so all she could do was fight the guards the best she could until somebody could come and help her.

All of Gabriell's friends were tied up fighting the guards, except for Courtney. While Courtney was watching her friends fight, she noticed that Gabriell was in terrible danger. She saw that Gabriell was getting beaten up. Courtney couldn't bear watching her friend get pounded by the men, so she ran over to the guards and Gabriell to help her. She knew that her chance of saving Gabriell was slim to nothing since she was so weak, but she had to try for her friend's sake.

At that moment, Courtney forgot about the poison in her body, that she wasn't strong enough to fight a guard or three guards at that. She didn't care because she saw that her friend was in danger and she just knew that she had to save Gabriell in some way or another.

"No, Courtney!" yelled Gabriell as she saw Courtney coming toward her.

Courtney ignored Gabriell's plea to not help her and went straight toward the men who were beating her up. She kicked the guards in the back as hard as she could. The guards stopped hurting Gabriell and turned around to see who kicked them. Then Gabriell saw that she had a chance to get away from the guards. She took it without hesitation.

The men saw that Courtney had hit them. One of the guards slapped her hard on the face for hitting them. Courtney went down to her knees and tried to get away from the guards.

"Courtney!" Gabriell yelled as she ran toward her friend who had just gotten hurt by one of the guards.

Gabriell went up to a man who was about to hit Courtney and threw a pot hard on his head. The guard fell down to the ground, and his friends went toward her.

"That's it! It will not let nobody hurt me and my friends anymore. You are both toast," Gabriell exclaimed, tired of the men tormenting her and her friends.

Gabriell wanted revenge on the two guards who hurt her and Courtney because she knew now that Courtney didn't have much of a chance of surviving until she got her the antidote. That's when Gabriell decided to end the fight once and for all and beat the two guards up without hesitation or sorrow, so she ran up to the men with a cane she found. She began to beat them up with all her might. She didn't stop hitting them until they were on the ground, knocked out cold.

Courtney's chance of surviving was slim now, thanks to the guards. Gabriell hoped and prayed that her friend would be okay. She was really starting to get worried about Courtney. Could she really get Courtney the antidote in time now?

"Are you okay?" Gabriell asked Courtney, looking down at her friend that had gotten hurt by one of the guards.

"Yeah, I guess so," Courtney said in pain while looking up at Gabriell's concerned face.

Courtney was starting to get very weak now that she had lost some of her strength by helping Gabriell. She would not last much longer without a cure. Gabriell hoped that Courtney still had enough strength to fight off the poison until she got her the antidote. She hoped that Courtney didn't use up all her strength trying to save her life.

"Thanks," Courtney said to Gabriell with a little smile.

"I should be thanking you," Gabriell said, worried about Courtney. "You saved my life when you are still in danger of not being okay."

"I know," said Courtney, understanding what she had done. "I just wanted to help you. I couldn't just watch you get beaten up."

"I know, and I appreciate it, but you didn't have to risk your life for me," Gabriell said to Courtney, concerned. "Now I will have a lesser chance of giving you the antidote in time."

"Don't worry," said Courtney, trying to cheer her friend up. "I still have enough strength left to survive until you can get me the antidote. I will be fine. Just worry about making a cure, not me."

"Okay, I'll do that," said Gabriell as she hugged her friend with fear in her eyes that Courtney wouldn't make it in the end. "Please let somebody carry you until we get to safety. You've got to save the rest of your strength to fight off the poison in your body."

"Okay," said Courtney, agreeing with Gabriell.

"Please, will one of you carry Courtney?" Gabriell asked her other friends, looking at each of them.

"I will," said Glenn as he knocked out the last guard.

"Thanks," Gabriell said as she smiled at Glenn.

"My pleasure," said Glenn to Gabriell with a little blush.

Glenn was starting to get sentimental toward Gabriell. Mike, Ayla, Erica, and Courtney noticed the slight change of face expression in Glenn's face, and they all softly giggled at each other.

Glenn picked up Courtney and carried her toward the exit of Slash's home. Then they all left Slash's house since the coast was clear. They were finally safe. They were all glad to be out of Slash's evil, creepy home, especially Gabriell and Courtney. They hoped and prayed that they would never see Slash again, which included people who reminded them of Slash. Unfortunately, there would always be bullies, like lovely Brain Escobach, who reminded them.

CHAPTER XX

Glenn and is friends were safe and sound in Mike's car. They had already informed the police that Slash Burns kidnapped Gabriell and Courtney, so the police were heading over to Slash's house to put him and his minions in jail where they belonged. They also told the police that Gabriell and Courtney were safe and to please inform their parents that they were okay and that they would be home soon. Glenn and his friends didn't inform the police about what had happened to Courtney in Slash's house because they didn't want to worry Courtney's parents.

They had a serious problem on their hands. They were three hours away from Gabriell's lab, which would only give Gabriell less than an hour to make the antidote for Courtney. That was not enough time for Gabriell to make a serum. She needed at least three hours. Glenn and his friends had to find a place besides Gabriell's lab to make the cure, but where would that be?

"Gabriell, we have to find a place in this town where you can make the antidote," said Mike, wanting to make sure that Courtney gets a serum in time.

"I know," said Gabriell, trying to think of a good place that would work perfectly.

"Hey!" said Erica, trying to get her friends' attention. "What about the hospital? Couldn't you make the antidote there?"

"I guess so, but what if the place is too crowded?" said Gabriell, worried that Erica's idea would not work. "What if all the labs in the hospital are filled up?"

"We will just have to take that risk," Mike persisted. "It's the only choice we got right now."

"Well, okay," said Gabriell, hoping that they would find the perfect place in the hospital to make the antidote Courtney needed.

"Do you all know where one is in this town?" Gabriell asked her friends. She hoped that one of her friends knew where a hospital was in Callington.

"Yes," said Glenn, thinking back into the past. "I think we saw one right before we had reached Dark Street."

"Do you remember where it is?" asked Gabriell.

"Yes," said Glenn, thinking back. "It seems like it was on Gale Street, which is ten minutes away from here."

"Great!" exclaimed Gabriell, glad to know that the hospital was close by. "Let's get this car moving!"

"You got it!" exclaimed Mike to Gabriell as he turned his face at her for a moment and smiled. Then Mike turned his head back toward the road and put the pedal to the metal. He wanted to get to the hospital as fast as he could. Mike did think about breaking the speed limit but decided against it. They needed all the time they could get to make the antidote for Courtney. They didn't have the time on their hands to talk to a police officer about speeding. That was all they needed.

Mike and his friends went through lots of traffic before they got to their destination. They reached the hospital when the ten minutes was up. They had made good time, even though the roads were all crowded with traffic.

Mike got off Gale Street and traveled onto the parking lot where Callington Hospital was. They hoped to find a good parking place so they wouldn't have to walk too far to get into the hospital. The parking lot didn't look too crowded, so everything was turning out good so far for Mike and his friends. They found a space that was only forty feet from the hospital, which wasn't too bad at all considering how big the place was.

Once they were parked, they all got out of Mike's car and walked straight toward Callington Hospital.

Callington Hospital was eight stories high. It was a big white building covered with lots of windows and a door here and there. In the windows, Mike and his friends could see patients in their rooms. People could usually see flowers standing close to the windows inside the patient's rooms. Most of the doors in and outside of the building were painted brown.

Inside the hospital, the walls were white and brown, and a few were pink and blue. It just depended on where people were in the hospital. Glenn and his friends happened to land in the lobby of the hospital.

The lobby was filled with brown carpet and white walls. There were a couple of soft cushioned chairs in the front end of the lobby next to some big windows. People would sit on those chairs to sit down and relax while waiting for somebody. Beside each chair was a desk covered with magazines, from *House & Gardening* to *Sports Illustrated*. At the back end of the lobby, there was an off-white counter with a lady and a man behind it.

The lady had short light-brown hair and grayish-brown eyes. She was short and chubby, while the man standing beside her was also short but not fat. He had glasses on over his light-yellow eyes, and he had a serious acne problem that was all over his face. The man also had long yellow hair to match his eyes. He was wearing a blue short-sleeve T-shirt with blue jeans to match, while the lady had a red blouse on with black overalls to match. She also had on a beautiful dark-red watch. The watch was decorated with beautiful butterflies and flowers. The second hand was followed by a butterfly. It seemed as if the butterfly was alive as it followed the second hand in the watch. The watch was a gift from her grandma. She loved the watch and cherished it as one of her favorite possessions.

The man and the lady stood behind the counter. They were waiting for someone to come up to them who needed help finding a patient, doctor, or nurse. Glenn and his friends went up to the lady and the man for help on where they could find a lab that they could use to make the antidote that Courtney needed.

"Can I help you?" the man asked Glenn and his friends as they approached the counter.

"Yes, my friend here got poison forced down her throat by someone," said Gabriell, trying to explain to the man why they needed his help. "I am a scientist that can make the antidote for her, but I need a lab that contains the ingredients I need for a cure."

"You are mighty young to be a scientist," said the man, becoming a little suspicious of Gabriell.

"I may be little young, but I am a true scientist. "My dad is a scientist. He taught me everything I know. I have been doing some experiments lately on energy myself. You may have heard about me and my experiments around town."

"What is your name then?" the man asked Gabriell.

"Gabriell San," said Gabriell to the man. She was getting tired of the man's questions.

"That name does sound familiar," said the man, thinking while scratching his head. "Well, okay, I guess that's proof enough for me. I'll check with a doctor to see if there is a lab open. He will probably be able to assist you if you need it. Please hold on one minute while I call to find out."

"Okay," said Gabriell, glad that she had finally gotten through to the man. "Thanks!"

The man went up to a phone behind the counter and picked up the receiver. Then he began to dial the number of one of the doctors who had a lab to themselves in the hospital. Once the number was dialed, he waited for an answer.

"Hello?" said a doctor who answered the phone.

"Hi, this is the office manager, Derek Solvan," said the man on the other line of the phone. "Is this Fred Vole?"

"Yes, it is," said Fred, identifying himself to Derek while wondering why he wanted him. "What can I help you with, sir?"

"A girl here says that she is a scientist that needs to make an antidote in a lab to save her friend," explained Derek.

"Hmmm, that's strange. We don't get people coming over here wanting to use the lab to help others," said Fred, thinking about the situation in hand.

"I know, but her friend is holding the hurt person right in front of me. I can't just watch her friend get sicker. This is a hospital for peep's sake," said Derek, not sure of what to think.

"I know, so why don't you send them to a room and let some doctors take a look at her friend. I am sure they can do much more for her than her friend can, even if she is a scientist," said Fred, not understanding the point Derek was trying to make.

"But that's just it, Doctor. She persist us to let her use a lab, and she does look like she is telling the truth. Besides, she says she's becoming a famous scientist around town."

"Famous, huh? Might be a scam. What is her name?" Fred asked Derek, wanting to make sure Gabriell was not lying about her identity.

"Her name is Gabriell San."

"I have heard of her before," Fred said, remembering a young doctor telling him about a girl who was becoming a great scientist, thanks to her father. "Tell her that my lab is open to her, and I would be glad to help her if she needs me."

"I'll do that," said Derek with a smile while he was getting ready to hang up the phone. "Thank you for your time and goodbye."

"Goodbye," said Fred, glad to help Gabriell.

"You may go to Fred's lab," said Derek to Gabriell with a smile. "It is on the second floor. Once you get there, go to the right. It is the third door you will see on your left. Fred should be waiting for you there to help you. That is if you need him since his shift is almost over for the day."

"Thank you," said Gabriell, pleased that Derek had found a lab that she could use to make the antidote Courtney needed in order to live.

Gabriell and her friends went to the elevator in the hallway that was across the lobby. Glenn pushed the button to go up and waited for the elevator to open. In a matter of seconds, the door was open. They squeezed into the elevator, and Mike pressed the button for the second floor. Once they had reached the second floor, they headed for Fred's lab.

The walls around them were blue, a calm color that was supposed to relax patients, but it didn't work all the time. There was also some pictures on the walls. They were of famous nurses and doctors who had worked at the hospital once before. Lights filled the hallway as Glenn and his friends walked toward Fred's lab. The floor didn't have a carpet on it. It was the plain color of white with lots of black squares on it.

Gabriell and her friends saw Fred's lab and went into it. Fred was inside the lab, waiting for them. He was wearing a big white coat that most scientists wear when they were doing experiments. He also had on a white long-sleeve shirt under the coat and white pants to match. Fred was very tall, about six feet and four inches. He was wearing a pair of glasses. Fred looked to be in his mid-thirties with short blond hair and dark-green eyes. Erica thought he looked handsome with his big, fancy white coat.

"Hi!" Fred said to Gabriell with a cheerful voice. He was wondering if Gabriell and her friends were the people who needed his lab and maybe his guidance. "Is one of you Gabriell?"

"Yes," said Gabriell as she stepped up away from her friends to greet Fred. "I am Gabriell."

"Nice to meet you, Gabriell," said Fred, glad to finally meet the young scientist in person. "My name is Fred Vole. I have heard about your new experiment. Are you getting anywhere with it?"

"Yes, I have gotten more out of that experiment than I could ever imagine, but right now, that doesn't matter. I must make a serum to save my friend," said Gabriell, thinking about what all they had been through to get to the hospital.

"Can I help you with anything then?" said Fred, wanting to help Gabriell.

"Yes," said Gabriell, glad that Fred had asked. "You can get the ingredients I need to make the antidote since you know where everything is."

"Great!" exclaimed Fred with a big smile on his face that touched his cheekbones.

Gabriell turned away from Fred and began to look around the lab. The first thing that caught her eye was a big white table with plenty of space on it to do experiments. It was in the middle of the lab on her right. She went up to the table and stood against it. Then she noticed that all the walls were covered with several potions and ingredients for the potions. They were in flasks, test tubes, bottles, and jars. They were all laid on shelves that were in rows, covering all the walls from top to bottom. Gabriell could barely see the color of the walls that were hidden by all the potions and ingredients for those potions. The walls were yellow. There was also a bed in the lab. It was lying against the back wall on Gabriell's right, the only empty space in the lab. Mike walked Courtney to the bed and laid her on it.

Courtney tried to relax as she waited for the antidote that she needed so desperately.

Courtney was getting very weak. Her face was very pale. It was as white as the snow that people see on those cold mornings in the winter. She also had a high fever. She was losing her strength fast. Gabriell only had about three hours to make the antidote for Courtney. Would that be enough time for Gabriell to make the antidote and give it to Courtney?

CHAPTER XXI

"Okay," said Gabriell, trying to think of the ingredients she needed to make the antidote. "I need magnesium and strontium for now," said Gabriell, picturing the antidote in Slash's hand before she had taken it to cure herself of the poison that was still in her best friend's body.

Fred got the two ingredients off the top-left shelf that was against the right wall, which was next to the table where Gabriell was standing at. Then he handed them to Gabriell. Gabriell looked at the ingredients for a moment and then poured them into a flask. Next, she stirred the magnesium and the strontium together. As she stirred those two ingredients together, Fred and her friends watched her. They knew that time was of the essence from here on out.

Once the two ingredients were mixed good, Gabriell told Fred the rest of the ingredients she needed. Then Fred went toward the shelves to gather the items. Some of the chemicals were on top of the shelves, and some were at the bottom.

Once Fred had found all the items that Gabriell needed, he laid it on the big wooden table beside her. Gabriell poured all the ingredients into separate bowls and stirred them good. Then she combined one ingredient at a time into a large bowl and stirred it carefully with a metal stick she had gotten from Fred. This took some time, but it was the only way to get the antidote done. If Gabriell had made the serum another way, it would have definitely failed. If something went wrong while Gabriell was making the antidote, Courtney would be dead by the time she made another batch for her. Gabriell knew this, so she had to make sure that she didn't make one mistake.

Gabriell made use of all the time she had to make the antidote since her friend's life was in her hands. Gabriell's friends, including Fred, watched her make a cure while Courtney rested on the bed. They were fascinated by Gabriell's talent. As they watched her work, they could see that she was going to be a great professor one day.

Courtney hoped that Gabriell would be finished with the serum soon because she wasn't sure how much longer she could last without it. The clock was ticking in the background. It showed that there was only about one hour left for Gabriell to finish making the antidote for Courtney. Gabriell heard the clock ticking, and while it was ticking its lovely tone, she wished that time would stand still until she had the antidote done for her friend. But of course, that didn't happen. Time could not be stopped, so she just had to do her best with the time she had left, but would it be enough?

Gabriell poured and stirred all the ingredients together, trying not to rush herself too much. She couldn't afford to make a mistake. Gabriell was too close to completing a cure. Then finally after stirring and pouring the ingredients together for thirty minutes, Gabriell finished the antidote. With a sigh of relief, she told everybody her work was done. Then she held a test tube high up into the air and poured the serum into it. She looked at the antidote for a moment, happy that it was finally completed. Then she carefully carried the cure to Courtney who was still on the bed, resting. Gabriell made sure that none of the antidote spilled on the floor.

Once Gabriell reached the bed, she looked at her best friend. Courtney's face was even whiter than it was before. Gabriell could tell by the look on her friend's face that she was struggling. Courtney only had twenty-five minutes left of life. Would that be enough time for the antidote to work? Gabriell thought as she looked at Courtney's face. She hoped that Courtney would be okay.

Twenty minutes had passed now. There was still no sign of the cure working. Gabriell and her friends were watching Courtney, searching for a sign of hope. They prayed that there was still a chance for the antidote to work.

Finally, after two more minutes had passed, the sign came. Courtney's face was turning back to normal right before their eyes. They watched the paleness in her face disappear and the same for the rest of her body. Gabriell touched her forehead and felt that Courtney's fever was finally gone. The antidote was working! Big smiles came over their faces as they watched Courtney come back to them. It was truly a miracle in the living.

As Gabriell and her friends saw that Courtney was finally going to be okay, they hugged her, and tears of joy started streaming down their faces. They were so happy to have her back. Gabriell saw now that she was a true scientist and that she had a wonderful talent.

"Thank you!" said Courtney to Gabriell, happy to be alive and to see all her friends' happy faces looking at her.

"You're welcome," said Gabriell, glad to see that her best friend was going to be A-OK. "How do you feel?"

"Much better, thanks to you," said Courtney with a smile while looking at all her friends' cheerful faces.

"No, you saved your own life," said Gabriell to Courtney. "I only helped."

"Yes, but without you, I wouldn't have made it," Courtney pointed out to Gabriell.

"I was just doing what I do best," Gabriell said to Courtney. She was very proud of herself.

"Well, keep it up."

"I will," Gabriell said with a smile that covered her whole face. "You don't have to worry about that. It's like you said. Science revolves around my whole life, so I might as well make use of it."

At that moment, Gabriell realized how important friends were to each other. She was so happy to have a true best friend. Gabriell didn't know what she would do without one.

Courtney stood up out of the bed and said that she was feeling great. She told everybody that she was ready to go home. All of Courtney's friends nodded their heads in agreement. Then they thanked Fred for letting them use his lab and waved goodbye to him as they left. Then Courtney and all of her friends went down the elevator, through the hallway and lobby, and out the hospital door. They were glad to finally be safe and sound once and for all.

CHAPTER XXII

Courtney and all of her friends travelled back to their homes. They would soon be at Gabriell's house. They couldn't wait to get to their own houses, especially Gabriell and Courtney.

They reached Gabriell's house at seven o'clock, right after supper. Gabriell jumped out of the car and ran toward the house while her friends followed behind her. She was so glad to finally be safe at her own home. She hadn't realized until now how much a person could miss their home. She glanced at her beautiful house for a minute and then went inside. She could not wait to see her mother's face.

Gabriell walked into the kitchen with her friends behind her. She looked around the kitchen to see if anything had change, but noting had. It was still the same old kitchen she had walked and ate in many times before. Then her mom came into the kitchen to see who had come into the house.

"Gabriell!" Diana exclaimed with joy as she ran over to her daughter and hugged her. "You're okay!"

Diana had the biggest smile on her face that anybody had ever seen when she hugged her daughter and held her tight for a minute. She was so glad to see Gabriell. Diana had missed her so much. She was also glad to see that all of Gabriell's friends were okay.

"I am fine," said Gabriell, happy to be in her mother's arms. "My friends saved me and Courtney."

"Thank you all so much," Diana said to Gabriell's friends, who were standing behind her.

"You're welcome, but Gabriell is the real one to thank," Ayla said to Diana, glad to see she was so happy to see her daughter. "We just helped."

"What do you mean?" Diana asked Ayla, a little puzzled.

"Let me explain," Courtney said as she stepped up in front of her friends. "Ayla and her friends saved us, but then Gabriell saved me. See the person that kidnapped us, Slash Burns, gave us a potion that really was poison, which would eventually kill us in eleven hours. Gabriell got the antidote from Slash and then made one for me. She used her talent to save my life."

"Gosh," Diana said, surprised, while looking at Courtney. "I had no idea. I am so glad that you all are okay, especially you, Courtney. It sounds like you went through a lot more than your friends went through in order to get her safely."

"I did," said Courtney, trying to stay cheerful as flashes of horrible memories of what she had just been through with all her friends went through her head.

"Is this Slash person in jail?" Diana asked Courtney and her friends, hoping that they were safe from that evil man once and for all.

"Yes, and hopefully, he will stay in jail forever because that is where he belongs," said Mike with a smile as he answered Diana's question, which didn't take him long at all to answer.

"Yes, it is," said Courtney and Gabriell. They were so glad to know that Slash was locked up in jail.

"Well, I am so glad that this story has a happy ending because I don't know what I would do without my daughter," said Diana as a tear was about to come out of her eye and roll down her face.

"It's okay, Mom," said Gabriell as she smiled at her.

"I know, darling," said Diana to her daughter. "Well, I better call Courtney's mom and tell her the good news. I'll make sure that Courtney gets home."

"Thank you," said Erica to Diana. "We better get going ourselves."

"Yes, you all go ahead and get home to your parents," said Diana to Gabriell's friends. "No need to keep them waiting. I am sure they are worried about you too."

"Yes," said Erica, thinking about her parents. "We will see you soon. Goodbye!"

"Goodbye!" said Diana, Courtney, and Gabriell as they waved to their friends. Then Diana went over to her phone and called Courtney's mom.

While Ayla and her friends were walking to Mike's car, they talked about the adventure they all just had together, the dangers they had faced and the guards they had beaten up with their special powers. They couldn't believe that it had all really happened, that they could have died in Slash's house or lost the battle against all the guards, and that they could have been stuck in that horrible house forever. But thank goodness that didn't happen and that everything turned out great in the end.

"That was quite an amazing adventure," Glenn said, recalling what had happened.

"Yes, it was," said Mike with a grin. "We tore those guards up, especially Slash!"

"Yeah, we're superheroes!" exclaimed Glenn, remembering everything that they had been through together. "The Special Ones!"

"Yes, those special powers really did help us save our friends and ourselves," Erica said, remembering. "Do you think the aliens knew that we would have to save our friends in order for them to be okay, and so they gave us special powers to help us on our quest?"

"Maybe," said Mike, thinking about Erica's question.

"If that is true, then what explains the nightmares we had had about the aliens, the strange bugs from outer space?" said Ayla, still puzzled about the dreams.

"Maybe the aliens were warning us to never go back to their spaceship because we would lose all our special powers and then we would not had been able to rescue our friends," Glenn guessed. "You know that spaceship may still be out there in the woods."

"Yeah, I guess you're right, Glenn," said Ayla, beginning to understand everything that had happened to them. All the pieces of the puzzles were finally fitting together for them.

"Wait a minute!" said Erica as everybody was about to get into Mike's car. Erica had just remembered something she had forgotten all about.

"I was supposed to be a student karate teacher today for Don," said Erica, disappointed that she had missed out on helping Don teach the class. "I have dreamed of such a day where I could be Don's partner in karate class. He is so cute, even though he is married and too old for me."

"Well, keep dreaming," said Ayla, about to laugh. "Besides, it wouldn't be fair for you to be his partner because you have that special power of yours. You can beat just about anybody in karate without practicing."

"I guess you're right, Ayla," said Erica, sadly agreeing with her friend. "Let's go home!"

"I'll say yes to that!" Glenn exclaimed, ready to get to his own house and go to bed. Glenn was tired and worn out from the long day he had with his friends, and they got in Mike's car and went home to their respective houses.

Meanwhile, Courtney was laughing about something that had happened while she and Gabriell were trapped in Slash's house.

"Hey, were you getting dibs on one of the guards that were fighting us in Slash's house right before we escaped?" said Courtney, anxious to hear her friend's reply.

"No, I wasn't!" said Gabriell, a little bit surprised by Courtney's question.

"Yes, you were!" said Courtney, remembering the way that Gabriell had looked at the guard.

"Okay, maybe I was," said Gabriell, admitting that Courtney was right. "I was just trying to get his attention so you could escape from him and get help."

"Yeah, right," said Courtney, doubting her friend.

"No, really," said Gabriell, trying to get Courtney to believe her.

"Uh-huh," said Courtney, laughing. "Sure you were."

www.ingramcontent.com/pod-product-compliance
Lightning Source LLC
LaVergne TN
LVHW09155006026
838200LV00036B/779